The Watching Eyes

Original title: The Winds of Time

by BARBARA CORCORAN

Illustrated by Bob Dacey

SCHOLASTIC BOOK SERVICES

NEW YORK · TORONTO · LONDON · AUCKLAND · SYDNEY · TOKYO

to Naomi Gates

Copyright © 1974 by Barbara Corcoran. This edition is published by Scholastic Book Services, a division of Scholastic Magazines, Inc., by arrangement with Atheneum Publishers. The book is entitled THE WINDS OF TIME in the edition published by Atheneum Publishers.

12 11 10 9 8 7 6 5 4 3 2   6 7 8 9/7 0 1/8

Printed in the U.S.A.

The
Watching Eyes

1

GAIL WOKE UP shivering, although the night was hot and sticky. The sheet that half-covered her felt damp, and she thought of shrouds and winding sheets and all those terms that sometimes haunted her dreams. Something was very wrong, but for a moment she could not remember what it was. Her big black-and-white cat, Sylvester, lay heavily across her feet. She remembered, then, what had happened and she sat up abruptly, jerking her feet out from under Sylvester who gave a mildly protesting mew.

Gail got out of bed and padded silently along the narrow hallway to her mother's room. She knew the room would be empty, but she felt the need to check and make sure. That afternoon while she was still in school, they had come for her mother again and taken her back to the mental hospital that she hated so. Five years ago, when Gail was eight, her mother had been there for seven-and-a-half months. Gail had stayed with her grandmother, but now her grandmother was dead. What would happen to her?

She turned the light on in her mother's room. It was a shambles. In the morning she would have to clean it up. Her mother was never very tidy; but when the sickness was coming on, she could make a room look as if a cyclone had just torn through it. It was one of the signs, and Gail had seen it coming for a long time. The increasing vagueness, the inability to remember what she ought to do, the frequent absences from her secretarial job, the feeling that the neighbors were spying on her; but, worst of all, the cold indifference toward Gail. That was the hardest to take, because when her mother was all right, she was warm and affectionate — an irresponsible mother, they said, but at least a mother you could laugh with and talk to, and give a good-night hug to. Gail's eyes burned with tears. She turned out the light, plunging the chaos of her mother's room into darkness.

Next door, Mrs. Abrams would be sleeping with one ear cocked to make sure Gail was all right. She had urged Gail to spend the night with her, but Gail had wanted to be alone. She had to think about what she was going to do. She must have some plan, because whatever the social worker came up with, she knew she wasn't going to like it. The only thing she could think of was to find her father. He had left when Gail was eight, just before her mother's first breakdown. She hadn't seen him since, but now and then he sent her a postcard, and he always said, "If you ever get into a jam, let me know." The trouble was that he moved around a lot, and sometimes he forgot to tell her where he was going. The last time she had heard from him, almost a year ago, he'd been in Honolulu. He was a painter, and her grandmother, his own mother, always said he was unreliable.

Gail went back to her own room and tried to settle down to sleep. I'll probably turn out to be unreliable, too," she said to Sylvester. "What can you expect with parents like mine?"

Sylvester turned over on his back, all four paws up in the air, waiting for her to rub his stomach.

"All I've really got is you," she said. The day before, the social worker had had a long talk with her, being terribly, offensively kind, as if Gail were some kind of walking wounded. And she had made a face that meant "Oh, how pathetic!" when Gail said she had no family now, except her father whose whereabouts she didn't know. But if that goggle-eyed woman had some kind of orphans' home in mind, she was off her rocker. Gail had decided she would run away first.

"Are you sure there's no one?" the worker had persisted. "It seems to me in the records there is something about a brother of your mother's...."

Remembering the conversation now, Gail turned cold and sick again. "Oh, him," she'd said quickly. "He can't do anything. He's way off somewhere in the Dakotas or somewhere." At once she was sorry she'd placed Uncle Chad even that definitely. "He doesn't like us," she added.

The social worker had peered at the fact sheet in front of her, her glasses slipping down her nose. "It says here, in case of need, contact brother, Chadwick Ashe. . . . There's an address here in Minot, North Dakota."

"He won't do anything." Gail had felt like screaming, or grabbing the piece of paper and tearing it up. Only probably there were five or six carbons somewhere. How *could*

4

her mother have given them Uncle Chad's name? It proved she really never had believed Gail about Uncle Chad.

She coaxed Sylvester up on the pillow beside her and put her arm around him. He purred loudly. "You're my only true friend," she told him. He opened his gold eyes and looked at her, and she would have been certain he understood her, if she hadn't known that at almost fourteen she was too old to believe things like that.

Uncle Chad. Her bachelor uncle. Her mother's only brother. A banker. Money. She knew the reason her mother refused to believe anything bad about him: he was the only one who had ever come through with money when they were broke. He had not come to visit them very often. For one thing, Gail's father had not liked him. But after her father had gone and her grandmother had died and her mother had just begun to act kind of strange again, he had come. He'd stayed a week, while Gail's mother went into the psychiatric ward at the hospital. He'd paid for everything and looked after Gail. Looked after her, all right.

She was nine then — or maybe ten; it was hard to remember. But, one awful night, the night before her mother had been discharged from the hospital, he had come into Gail's room to tell her he was going to take her to Minot. He'd tried to make it sound like a big deal, but she knew what he had in mind; he wanted a free housekeeper, a slave. When she'd accused him of that, he had yelled at her and his face had turned all purple. She had yelled back. Then he had hit her hard on the arm, and he said she and her mother had better show some gratitude. Again she had talked back to him, and he had hit her on the side of the head. He looked like a wild man. Her ear had pained her and she had felt a ringing in it. Scared, she had grabbed a book and thrown it at him. It had hit him on the nose and given him a nosebleed. Swearing, he had slammed out of the room. She had put a chair under the doorknob so he couldn't open it, and she had stayed awake all night. In the morning he was gone.

When her mother came home, she kept talking about how good Uncle Chad had been, how grateful they should be. Finally, Gail had had to tell her, but it had been a mistake. Her mother had gone into a screaming fit and called Gail a liar. Gail had had to call the doctor to give her a sedative. They never spoke of Uncle Chad again and he never came back, although sometimes he sent her mother some money.

"I would rather die," Gail said to Sylvester, as she lay awake, remembering all that. "I don't want to be anywhere near him."

There was really no reason, she thought, why anybody had to make any arrangements for her. She was nearly grown up, after all, and for a long time she had been doing everything around the house, the cooking and cleaning and all, even looking after the money. Her mother got nervous about money, so she turned the checkbook over to Gail. Each week Gail figured out what bills they could pay, wrote the checks, and all her mother did was sign them. In the last few months Gail had stashed away part of the grocery money each week, just in case the going got rough again. And now it was rough, all right. But if they'd just let her alone, she could manage fine, even keep on going to school. It seemed so reasonable that she began to feel it might really turn out that way. She knew how to manage meals on practically no money. "Just cat food for you, and some hamburger and vegetables and milk for me," she told Sylvester. She'd use that dry milk, and pick up lettuce and stuff at the market just after it began to wilt; she'd often done that, and they usually gave it to her or charged her practically nothing. Hamburger was getting pretty expensive —

7

maybe chicken would be better. "And there's always soybeans," she said. She had studied nutrition charts and knew food values. Her mother said she was a wonderful manager.

In the street outside her window a siren wailed, and she got up to look. Not that a siren in that neighborhood was any big thing, but she was awake and it was something to do. She watched the whirling red light on top of the police car as it screamed down the street. After somebody. She knelt on the floor, her chin propped on her hands. Across the street the neon sign on Clancy's Bar blinked on and off, the second *c* in Clancy missing. Further down the street was her friend Kristin's father's gas station. The sign of the Flying Red Horse. When she was little, she had urged her father to buy Mobil gas because she thought if they offered up this sacrifice to the Flying Red Horse, he might some day let her get on his back and fly off to the stars. Flying off to the stars had been her major goal for a long time.

Across the street two drunks supported each other, staggering along the sidewalk, stopping to argue from time to time. Drinking was stupid. Drugs were stupid. It was hard enough to survive when you had your head together; and if there was one thing

Gail was determined to do, it was to keep her head together. In school, earlier in the week, her history teacher had complained that young people ignored the past. But what Mrs. Jenkins didn't understand was that the present was just about all a kid could cope with nowadays. Mrs. Jenkins was about a thousand years old, and she'd probably grown up on some grassy farm someplace in the Middle West, where all you had to worry about was if the cows got lost. But this was Now, and this was the City, and you'd better be with it or you'd be dead.

Shivering a little in the damp, warm air, she got back into bed and pulled the sheet up to her chin. Sylvester resettled himself in the crook of her knees, purring. Finally, to the sound of night traffic, she fell asleep.

2

WHEN SHE GOT HOME from school, the social worker was there, lying in wait. Gail had tried hard to be tolerant of Miss Bullitt, telling herself that the woman must mean well or she wouldn't be a social worker. But her tolerance was constantly being strained to the breaking point. The worst thing was Miss Bullitt's patronizing manner, her air of a queen bestowing wisdom and largess. And the second worst thing was her teeth. They stuck way out — they came at you like a dragon's teeth. Sometimes you got the feeling you couldn't escape them; you would be ground into little pieces by those teeth and sold as hamburger to raise money for the starving children of some far country. Gail had tried to tell herself there could be a worse fate; but however she looked at it, she always came back to the feeling of being painfully shredded.

The social worker who had come the last time her mother got sick had been wonderful. A beautiful, young black woman, with real sympathy. You could tell her anything, and she'd understand. But she had disappeared — transferred, Miss Bullitt had said, making it sound as if she had been demoted.

"Well, dear, are you getting along all right?" Miss Bullitt asked, flashing those terrible teeth.

"Fine, thank you," Gail said, warily.

"I checked with the hospital this morning." She paused and consulted her notebook. "Dr. James feels that it may be . . . I'm sorry, dear . . . quite some time before your mother is ready to come home."

Gail nodded, not surprised. Mom had been in bad shape this time. Gail knew all the degrees of the sickness, all the manifestations.

"Do you feel, dear, that you can manage for a few days, until we can make some arrangement? Mrs. Abrams has agreed to keep an eye on you."

"I don't need an eye on me."

Miss Bullitt smiled kindly. "I know you must feel quite grown up. But you are, you see, a minor, and will be for some years yet. Steps have to be taken."

11

Gail eyed her warily. "What kind of steps?"

Miss Bullitt gave her a mysterious smile, like someone who has been asked to divulge what one is going to get for Christmas. "We're working on it. Believe me, we have your interests at heart."

"I can really manage by myself," Gail said. "I mean if the law says you have to check up on me, you could drop in once in a while, but I am perfectly all right. I've been managing the house for a long time."

Miss Bullitt sucked air in an offer of commiseration. "I am sure it's been very hard for you."

"No, not hard at all," Gail said. "I get along fine."

Miss Bullitt rose "I'll be in touch with you in a few days, Gail. Meanwhile, please notify Mrs. Abrams if you need anything, or if you have to be out of the house other than during school hours."

"You mean I have to report in, whenever I go anywhere?" Gail couldn't believe it; for years she had come and gone as she pleased.

"For the time being, yes." Miss Bullitt waved an airy wave. "I'll be in touch."

When she had gone, Gail went to the kitchen and got out the butter dish from the back of the closet. She took out a carefully folded wad of bills and counted them. Twenty-three dollars. It wasn't much; but if things came to the point where she had to split, it would start her on her way. She put the dish back, hiding it behind the plastic fruit-juice pitcher and the cut-glass sherbets that her grandmother had left her. Cut-glass sherbets; how unreal could you get! She wondered what her grandmother had had in mind. Had she seen Gail presiding at beautiful, formal dinners in a hundred-thousand-dollar home, gazing down the length of the snowy damask tablecloth (there was a damask tablecloth, too, that Grandmother had left), silver gleaming in the candlelight, crystal clinking, and, to top it all off, the cut-glass sherbets full of . . . what? Jello, she thought derisively. Who did Grandmother think she was? Some future executive's smiling wife? First lady of the land? Governor's wife? Well, she didn't intend to be anybody's wife, and to heck with cut-glass sherbets and the whole bit. She'd eat yogurt out of the carton and like it.

At school that week it was hard to keep her mind on her work. No one, as far as she could tell, knew that her mother had gone to the hospital, not even Kristin, who was her only even halfway friend. When she first went to the high school, both girls and boys had tried to be friendly, but she had frozen them out. She didn't really mean to, but that was the way she was and she couldn't help it; she didn't trust people. If you trusted people, the first thing you knew they deserted you, or tried to turn you into a slave, or got sick and turned against you, or left you a bunch of cut glass. You couldn't count on people.

So she said nothing to Kristin about her mother, and she made excuses to avoid having Kristin come home with her. A couple of times she went to Kristin's house, deliberately not informing Mrs. Abrams in advance. But Mrs. Abrams was a good, motherly soul, who didn't press her.

Then, one afternoon, Gail came home to find Miss Bullitt waiting for her, looking like some old cat that had swallowed some dumb canary. And I'm probably the dumb canary, she thought, looking at her suspiciously.

"Dear Gail," Miss Bullitt purred. "Such good news!"

"Is Mama coming home?"

Miss Bullitt waved her hand in a gesture that seemed to say "oh, much better than *that*." "It's a surprise, but you're going to be very happy. You're a lucky girl."

"Is Mama better?"

"No, I'm afraid not. I told you the doctor's prognosis: it will be a long pull. But cheer up, dear, Someone Up There is really looking after you. You run upstairs and wash up and put a few things in a bag. . . ." Miss Bullitt went to the window and peered out.

"You'd better tell me," Gail said. "I hate surprises." She couldn't remember a surprise for years that had turned out any good, except last Christmas when she and her mother had celebrated by having hot pastrami sandwiches at Mandel's and going to a funny little place where they showed old movies. They'd seen *Some Like It Hot*, which Gail had really enjoyed.

Without turning around, Miss Bullitt said, "Wait a minute. Wait just a minute, dear."

Gail tried to look out the window, but she couldn't see past Miss Bullitt's mop of muddy-brown hair. "Is it Miss Blake?" she asked. When she'd been transferred to another district, Miss Blake had said she'd drop by, if Gail and her mother had any bad problems.

Miss Bullitt turned, frowning. "Agatha? No, of course not. What would she be doing here?"

"Well, I just thought . . . ."

"This is my district." Miss Bullitt pushed past Gail as someone knocked lightly at the door. Before she got there, the door opened.

"Anybody home?" It was a man's voice, and for one wild moment Gail thought it might be her father. But at once, even before she saw who it was, she knew. It was Uncle Chad.

He pushed the door further open and came in, smiling his broad, friendly smile, looking so much like what he was in his expensive tweed suit and his fashionable tie that, for a moment, even Gail could hardly believe her own memory. No wonder her mother hadn't believed her. No one ever looked less like a child hitter than Uncle Chad. He was the picture of prosperous, respectable, good-looking, physically fit Executive America. If you had a brother like that, you wouldn't want your child telling you mean things about him.

"Gail, honey!" He held out both hands. "It's been a long, long time."

She nodded, not moving toward him. "Hi, Uncle Chad."

After a second he let his hands drop. "It's good to see you, little niece."

"She's so surprised," Miss Bullitt gushed, obviously impressed by this handsome man.

"I didn't tell her, just as you said."

Still looking at Gail, he said, "Good for you, Miss Bullitt." He smiled sadly. "Honey, I'm so sorry about your mother."

She eyed him warily. She didn't think he cared all that much. He just wanted a free slave he could beat on when he felt mean. She'd seen men like that on TV. If you complained, they'd tell everybody you were crazy. "Like her mother," Uncle Chad would say. And people would tell her she was so lucky, she must be awfully grateful for her great, marvelous uncle. And all the time she'd be scrubbing floors, cooking huge meals, and hanging out washing, like Cinderella or something.

"My sis and I were always very close," Uncle Chad said.

"I knew you must be," Miss Bullitt said. "She mentioned you — obviously devoted. That's why I got in touch with you, Mr. Ashe."

He nodded. "Good judgment, Miss Bullitt. Sound judgment. Gail, honey, I've been to see your mother, and I've got the proper authorization from the court. I flew out here as soon as Miss Bullitt called me, but I've rented a car. So why don't you get together what you'll need. Don't bother about a lot of clothes; we'll take care of all that when we get there."

"Get where?" Gail's teeth were clenched.

Miss Bullitt and Uncle Chad exchanged glances. "Your uncle is taking you to North Dakota, honey," Miss Bullitt said. "Isn't that lovely?"

"I won't go."

"She hasn't seen me for a long time," Uncle Chad said. "We should have prepared her, I guess. It was my fault; I was so anxious to surprise her."

"Oh, I suppose it is a bit of a shock. But a happy shock, I'm sure." Miss Bullitt beamed at Gail.

Sylvester came out of the shadows and leaned against Gail's leg, purring. She reached down and touched him. "I'm not going."

Miss Bullitt sighed. "My dear, it's all settled. The judge has signed the court order."

"When we get home, I'll take out adoption papers." Uncle Chad looked at her as if he were offering her the moon. His face, his iron-gray hair, his even white teeth . . . ("My brother Chad has all his own teeth," her mother said. "Never had a cavity in his life. Can you imagine?"), his kindly smile, his horn-rimmed glasses. Gail looked at him, risking a direct eye-to-eye stare. Her mother did love him, and she'd say Gail was wrong. But her grandmother hadn't trusted him, and her father despised him. They must have known what he was really like. Mama must have known too; but she could put things out of her mind if it were more convenient that way. She liked his gifts of money. As Gail looked at him, she saw the little warning glitter of anger in his dark eyes. Do as I say, it said, or I'll beat you bloody.

She bolted for the door. But Uncle Chad was too fast for her. His fingers dug into her arm and he wasn't smiling now. "I have a court order," he said.

Gail knew what a court order was. For the moment she was defeated. "I won't go without my cat," she said.

He frowned, then shrugged. "I don't happen to like cats, but I won't be unreasonable. Bring him along. We'll cope with the problem when we get home."

Gail could imagine how he'd cope.

"There, dear," Miss Bullitt said. "How fortunate you are! An uncle who thinks of your wishes. Oh, this is going to mean so much to your mother, to know you're safe with your uncle." With an edge of threat in her voice, she said, "I wouldn't want to have to tell her there was any trouble."

Gail couldn't bear to think of old Bullitt upsetting her mother on her account. She would go with Uncle Chad, for now. But before she got to Minot, she would run away.

3

WHEN SHE CAME into the room with her battered suitcase and with Sylvester on a leash, Miss Bullitt and Uncle Chad stopped talking. Miss Bullitt flashed a big false smile at her.

"My, you were quick! All ready for your great adventure?"

Gail ignored her. She had enough to do, trying to make herself go with Uncle Chad. All the time she'd been packing, she had kept telling herself that she was a big girl now; she could take care of herself. But she was frightened. What if there were no way to escape?

Uncle Chad took her suitcase. "You'll lock up and attend to everything?" he said to Miss Bullitt.

"Yes, indeed. Don't you worry about a

thing. Gail, drop me a pretty postcard when you get there."

"Oh, we'll be in touch," Uncle Chad said. He held out his hand. "Thank you for everything, Miss Bullitt. If this troubled nation of ours had more such dedicated public servants. . ."

Miss Bullitt's mouth trembled with emotion and her jutting teeth seemed to quiver. "We do what we can," she said.

As they went down the walk, a familiar-looking Volkswagen drove up. Gail caught her breath. "It's Miss Blake!" Maybe she'd be saved.

"What does she want?" Miss Bullitt said sharply. To Uncle Chad, she said, "She used to have your sister's case." She shook her head, frowning, to convey her disapproval of Agatha Blake.

Maybe it was a sign, a last-minute reprieve. Tugging Sylvester behind her, Gail hurried to the VW. "Miss Blake!"

"Hi, Gail." The tall young woman got out of the car and held out her hand. "I heard you were leaving. I came by to say goodbye."

"Gail's uncle is in rather a hurry," Miss Bullitt said coldly.

"I want to talk to Miss Blake," Gail said.

"I'm not going anywhere till I talk to Miss Blake."

"Really, Agatha," Miss Bullitt said, "this is not your concern, you know."

Miss Blake smiled at Miss Bullitt. "Gail is a friend of mine. It's a matter of personal concern, Jennie, not professional." She took Gail's arm. "We'll be right back." She nodded to Uncle Chad, who looked annoyed, and walked Gail down the sidewalk toward Clancy's Bar and the sign of the Flying Red Horse.

"I'm so sorry about your mother." Miss Blake had a nice voice. "But you must try not to worry. I'll look in on her and keep you posted." She got a pen and a small pad from the pocket of her jacket. "What's your uncle's address?"

Gail gave it to her. "But I may not be there long."

"Why not?"

Gail struggled to tell her friend, but she couldn't do it. How could you say your own uncle was a wicked man? Mama would never forgive her if she said that. "I don't like him."

Miss Blake searched her face. "Your mother does."

"I know."

"It won't be for long, I'm sure. Your

mother always gets better sooner than they expect."

"It will be forever. He's going to adopt me." She looked at Miss Blake with such despair that Miss Blake stopped on the sidewalk.

"Honey, is it something we ought to know about? What is it that's wrong?"

Miserably Gail stared up at the red horse, his wings spread, just above them. If only she could get on his back and go far, far away. She shook her head. "I'll manage, I guess."

Miss Blake gave her arm a quick squeeze. "Any port in a storm, sweetheart. You're a good, strong girl. You'll cope." She tore off a piece of paper and wrote something on it. "This is my phone number. If things get rough, give me a ring."

Behind them, Uncle Chad impatiently blew the horn of the rented Pontiac, and Miss Bullitt called, "Yoo hoo! Gail! Agatha!"

They turned and walked back to the car. Gail got into the front seat and hauled Sylvester up into her lap. He wasn't crazy about riding in a car, but he put up with it. She buried her face in his neck to hide the desperation she knew must show. Uncle Chad thanked Miss Bullitt, and Miss Bullitt thanked Uncle Chad. As the car pulled away from the curb, Gail looked at Miss Blake and waved. Her eyes were blinded by tears, but she knew Miss Blake waved back. Gail touched the little leather purse inside her shirt pocket, where she had Miss Blake's phone number and the twenty-three dollars in grocery money. That and Sylvester were all she had.

4

"IT LOOKS LIKE a storm."

Gail opened her eyes. She had had them closed for some time, partly so Uncle Chad would think she was asleep and not try to talk to her, partly because she was concentrating on memorizing Miss Blake's number. She had it in her purse, but a person could lose her purse. She had long ago memorized her father's last address. Too bad she couldn't somehow get the twenty-three dollars inside her mind for safekeeping too, she was thinking when Uncle Chad said that about a storm.

The sky was layered with dark clouds and streaks of light. Down near the horizon the sky looked green. In spite of herself, Gail was interested in the look of the country. She had never been more than a few miles out-

side her own city. They had come up out of
the rolling hills and meadows into the west
side of the mountains. There were tall stands
of evergreens on one side of the road, and a
fast-moving stream, clear and almost golden
in the peculiar light, ran along the other side.

Gail sat way over by the door, her cat
pulled up close to her. Sylvester slept lightly,
opening his eyes a little at any unaccustomed
sound. Now he turned his head and looked at
her. When she rolled down the window to
the bottom, he leaned his chin on the frame.
The wind flattened the black cap of fur on
the top of his white head.

"I hope you won't get too tired," Uncle
Chad said. "I'm going to drive right through
to Minot. I'm anxious to get home. I have a
lot of work at the bank waiting for me. You
can sleep all right there, can't you?"

"Yes." She glanced at him out of the corner
of her eye. So they wouldn't be stopping at a
motel. That was bad. She had been planning
to get away after he went to sleep. It had
worried her because she had no idea where
the motel would be or what kind of town
she'd have to cope with. Well, now she could
forget that. If he stopped the car anywhere
during the night, for gas or anything, she'd
jump out and make a run for it. She shivered,

27

imagining herself and Sylvester fleeing across strange, wild country in the dark, with Uncle Chad after them. Gail decided she must escape as soon as they came to a city big enough to hide out in. If he didn't stop, she'd tell him she had to go to the bathroom. Then she'd get away somehow. But all this wild country with no cities in it made her nervous. What if there weren't any cities between where they were and Minot?

It grew colder as they went higher into the mountains. She closed her window. Uncle Chad turned on the radio, but it was mostly static, and after a while he shut it off. He was driving fast. She shrank against the door as a big lumber truck roared past them. The enormous logs looked as if they were held on the truck with Scotch tape or something, and she held her breath as the truck cut in front of them and the logs shifted slightly.

Uncle Chad smiled. "Scare you?"

She didn't answer.

"You probably wonder why we didn't fly home. Well, I flew out and I'm not all that fond of flying." He paused. "I flew a fighter plane in World War II, you know."

She nodded. Of course she knew. Her mother had a big framed picture of Uncle Chad in his flying helmet and fleece-lined jacket, leaning against the little plane that had five x's painted on the side. The x's were for German planes he'd shot down. Uncle Chad was a war hero, with medals to prove it and a piece of flak in his leg, so he said.

"I got enough of it in the war," he said. "I mostly stay away from planes now." He grinned. "All I've got to show for it is a lousy temper."

She tried to think about him objectively — the brother her mother admired; the brother-in-law her father despised and her grandmother distrusted; the war hero, the banker, the child beater. What kind of a man could be all those things?

She went back to thinking about escaping. She'd be entirely on her own; she couldn't appeal to sympathetic-looking strangers, because the minute they found out Uncle Chad had a court order, she'd be sunk. Court orders carried the final weight; she'd found that out the first time her mother had been committed to the hospital. You couldn't argue with court orders.

The car came around a curve in the road, into a steep-sided canyon that shut out most of the late afternoon light. It was a scary place, like being at the bottom of some awful pit. She tried not to look up at the cliffs that held them in.

Then, suddenly, they were in a town, a

tiny town only about four blocks square, with dark, ugly buildings jammed close together. The only thing she could bear to look at was the broad, clean river, flowing along the far side of the town. Uncle Chad pointed out a mine on the side of the hill across the river.

"I guess nobody'd live here," he said, "if it weren't for the mines. Lots of silver around here." He pulled up in front of a dingy little café and bar. "We'd better get some supper. Towns are few and far between."

She hesitated a moment but she *was* hungry, and anyway you could never escape a trap like this town. She got out, opened the window a crack for Sylvester, and followed her uncle into the smoky café. She ordered a hamburger and a carton of milk. Uncle Chad, flirting with the waitress, ordered a steak. He went into the bar and came back in a few minutes, a shot glass of bourbon in one hand and a glass with ice in it in the other. He poured the bourbon over the ice and added water.

Smelling the bourbon, Gail remembered something she had forgotten: on that night, long ago, Uncle Chad had smelled of whiskey. It made her feel so sick, she wasn't sure she could eat. And it frightened her. Did it take whiskey to get Uncle Chad into a beating-up mood?

When her hamburger came, she ate it quickly, then took the milk out to Sylvester. She snapped on his gold leash and walked him down by the river. If she could only get away! She wondered if he had stopped in this town on purpose, knowing there was nowhere she could run to. She passed a tiny office with a Greyhound bus sign, but there was no bus anywhere around.

While Sylvester daintily lapped up his milk and then chased a butterfly, she stared at the swift river, trying to keep calm. Panic was the one thing she mustn't do.

She heard Uncle Chad toot the horn. With a sigh, she picked up Sylvester and went back to the car.

In the car, Uncle Chad put an opened pint of bourbon into the glove compartment and started off, up the winding canyon road.

He left the radio on, although it was mostly a blare of static. Gail was glad he did because it ruled out conversation. She leaned against the door and closed her eyes, trying to imagine what was going to happen to her. She hoped when she ran, Sylvester wouldn't be a problem. She'd have to carry him, because he never was too cooperative about going where she wanted him to go, especially if she were in a hurry. She knew it had been foolish to bring him, but she'd had him since he was a kitten; he was almost like a part of herself. When she was little, her mother used to say he was magic. Once she'd gazed into his unblinking eyes and made three wishes but they never came true, and she knew right then that magic was a lot of nonsense, like horoscopes and Santa Claus.

She bent her head to look at Sylvester's golden eyes. He stared back at her sleepily. She wished he *were* magic. Then she'd make three wishes, all of them the same: let me get away from Uncle Chad. But wishing didn't make things happen. You had to look after yourself. She'd learned that a long time ago.

Evening came early in the canyon, even in early June, a kind of cold twilight gray. On either side the forest seemed to lean toward them, shutting out light, threatening. The air had grown sharp. Uncle Chad turned on the heater. Gail tried to think what it must have been like to come through there in a covered wagon, with no road or anything. How cold and frightening it must have been! Her great-great-grandfather had come out West from New England to mine for gold, but he'd never found much. Her mother had some of the letters he'd written home. They were not very interesting; mostly he'd written his wife to remember to pay George Dodge the twenty dollars they owed him, and to be sure his son Walter cut the hay in time, and to sell the horse if she thought it best. Then at the end he might say something casual, like, "I'm sending you fifty dollars in gold by Wells Fargo today." Most of the time, though, Gail didn't like to think about old things and dead people. They didn't have anything to do with her.

In spite of her determination to stay awake, she finally dozed, tired from the long tense day. She woke up with a start, her head banging against the window glass. They were out of the canyon, coming down on the eastern side of the mountains.

"It's snowing," Uncle Chad said.

5

SHE WAS STARTLED into answering him. "Snowing! How could it be?" Only that morning at home she had awakened early, too hot to sleep.

"It's the altitude," he said. "Once you get up here in the Rockies, anything can happen, weather-wise." Then he told her a long story about getting stuck in a snowdrift in July. Gail didn't believe a word of it. And yet it really was snowing. The windshield wipers squeaked and moaned, trying to keep the windshield clear. Uncle Chad reached down and put on the defroster. "Hand me that bottle in the glove compartment, will you, honey?"

She hesitated, but when he started to reach for it himself, she gave it to him and watched him take a long gulp from the bottle. He put it on the seat between them.

"Might as well keep it handy." He laughed, a funny kind of giggle. She wondered if he were getting drunk. Maybe he'd pass out, and she could dump him in the snow and drive away with Sylvester. She didn't have a license but she'd driven her mother's car a few times, before the finance company took it away.

The car skidded a little as they came down a hill, and a little later a car coming toward them slewed around a corner and almost hit them.

"You've got to know how to drive in the mountains," Uncle Chad said. "It's an art." He reached for the bourbon again. "Want a little? It'll warm the cockles of your heart."

"No, thank you," she said.

For a while he drove in silence, concentrating on seeing where he was going. The silent snow whirling around the car upset Gail. She felt trapped again. Sylvester stirred and sat up, his nose against the window. He also seemed tense, his ears pricked nervously forward, his tail twitched slowly back and forth. It was a bad night.

They went through a town where only the streetlights and an occasional night light in a gas station showed. It must be later than she thought, or else people in mountain towns went to bed early. It was strange to see a town dark and blanketed with snow at that time of year.

They came finally to a small city, where Uncle Chad stopped on the eastern edge of town to buy gas. This was the kind of situation Gail had planned for, to make her escape, but it was obviously impossible. Almost everything had closed for the night, and in the pitch dark and the ominous swirling snow, she wouldn't even be able to see where she was going. She prayed that they were not yet near Minot. She didn't think they could be. She had looked at it once on the map and it seemed a long way off. As soon as it got light and stopped snowing, she looked for an escape.

Uncle Chad got out and spoke to the sleepy attendant. They talked about the storm.

"It won't last," the man said. "Not this time of year."

Uncle Chad paid him, and they drove on, out into the country again. They went up a long hill and started down the other side. The snow suddenly began to thin, and it was possible to see at least a few yards ahead. Dense stands of pine were eerily white with the unseasonable snow. They passed a dirt road and Gail wondered where it went.

Uncle Chad had a drink and asked her to put the cap back on the bottle. When she had done it, he said, "That's a good girl. We're going to be friends, Gail — wait and see if we aren't." He reached over and patted her knee. Instantly, Sylvester flashed out a white paw and left a long red scratch on Uncle Chad's hand.

Uncle Chad jerked back his hand and swore, and at the same time the car swerved and went into a skid. For what seemed like years, they slid down the road sideways. Uncle Chad fought the wheel and almost got it under control. But the car got away from him again, slid off the road in a slow, sickening dive and turned over, driver's side down.

Gail bumped her head hard on the steering wheel. She was thrown almost on top of Uncle Chad and, as she fought to get free, she realized that he was not moving. She found the flashlight that she had seen in the glove compartment and turned it on him. He was unconscious, his head bleeding, one arm twisted under him. Sylvester was pawing furiously at the door that was now above Gail. After a struggle, she got it open and Sylvester leaped out. She scrambled out after him and saw him run back up the hill.

"Sylvester! Wait!" But he didn't slow

down. Wanting to follow him, to leave while she had the chance, but not ready to abandon even Uncle Chad in that condition, she hesitated, keeping her eye on Sylvester until he was almost out of sight in the darkness and the snow. Just then a car came toward her. She signaled frantically with her flashlight until the car passed her. It slowed, stopped, and backed up. She shone the light into the ditch where the rented car lay, its right wheels still spinning slowly. Then she turned off the flashlight and ran.

She ran, slipping and falling and running again, until she came to the road she had noticed. Gail turned down it, and as soon as she was far enough off the main road to risk a light, she turned the flashlight toward the ground. Sure enough, there were Sylvester's paw prints in the light covering of snow. She switched off the light and ran on down the road.

She passed a fork in the road, stopped, and turned back. Again the paw prints, this time taking the turnoff, a narrow road that pitched sharply down and then straightened out, with a stone wall on the right and an open area beyond it. She stood still and tried to see what was in there. The last slow flakes of the snowstorm whirled in her face, tossed around by a sudden wind. Gail thought she heard Sylvester's hoarse mew and strained to listen. She tried the light again, but the quick wind had obliterated his tracks. She heard him again, farther away, but definitely on the other side of the stone wall. Tucking the light under her arm, she climbed the rough wet stones and slid down the other side. The light banged against the wall.

"Sylvester!" She called him and waited, but the only sound now was the high moan of the wind. She moved forward, stopped, tried the light. It didn't work. She shook it and tried again. No luck! She touched the glass and cut her finger. The glass and the bulb had broken when she climbed the wall. Gail was frightened and had no idea where she was, nor where Sylvester had gone. She couldn't see a thing, except dark looming shapes that might be trees or might be anything. She was shivering violently.

With rising panic, she thought, "I could die here. I could freeze to death and never even be found." She thought of the car that had stopped. If they looked for her, they might see her footprints. But then she remembered how the wind had covered Sylvester's prints. And with all the excitement of finding Uncle Chad and getting him taken care of, it would be a while before they'd even remember to look for her.

She could go back. There would still be somebody there, probably — a cop or a wrecking car or something. But they would return her to Uncle Chad, if he were still alive. She didn't think he would die; he hadn't looked that bad. Just knocked out, and maybe that arm broken. She took a deep, shaky breath and decided she'd rather stay where she was and take her chances than go back to him.

She heard Sylvester again, she was sure of it. Gail started to run. Suddenly, she stepped into empty space, fell, and hit hard on a solid bottom. Stunned for a minute, she lay still, her head spinning. Then she turned and looked up. She was in some kind of big basin in the ground, and just above her head a round face, like the face of a baby, looked down at her. Gail screamed.

6

SHE COULDN'T HEAR the sound of her own scream above the wind. Her hair whipped around her face, and for a moment she crouched in the hole where she had fallen, her arms over her head to protect her from whatever was there.

Then, bracing herself for horror, Gail took her arms away from her face and looked. She let her breath out in a shuddering sigh of relief. The face was part of a marble Cupid, set on a chipped block of granite. She scraped the snow from the floor of the hole, exposing faded and flaking blue paint. She had fallen into an empty ornamental pool. Shakily, she stood up and tried to see what was around her. Just beyond the pool, a marble bench was tipped over. She walked carefully around it, limping a little from the bruises the fall into the pool had given her.

She was in a formal garden, with paths and evergreens that had once been trimmed but now had grown straggly. She walked cautiously along what seemed to be the main path. Maybe there would be a deserted house or even a tool shed where she could get in, out of the cold wind.

In the distance she could see the pale blur of the forest, the trees still covered with snow. It was a spooky place to be. She wondered about wild animals and then tried not to think of them. She didn't think there were wolves anymore, but there could be bears, coyotes, and wildcats. Would they attack you? She had always lived in a city; now she wished she had paid more attention to nature. If she were going to hide out here for while, she would have to depend on nature to help her out. It was silly to be scared, she told herself; everybody said a city street was more of a jungle than the wildest forest, and she had never been afraid of the city. But she was used to it. Being used to it was what helped.

Suddenly she was out of the formal garden. Beyond her, set down in a hollow surrounded by trees, was an enormous house, three stories high, with gables and turrets thrusting up into the night sky. The house was dark, although after a moment Gail thought she saw a light on the ground floor. But it moved, like a firefly, and she decided it was her imagination, or perhaps actually a firefly trapped inside the house. She started toward it, hoping she could find some way to get in out of the cold. Uncle Chad would never find her here. Even if he found the house, it was so big, she could surely find a place to hide.

Out of the darkness two pale shapes leaped at her. With a cry, Gail jumped backward, stumbled, and fell. Instantly the shapes were upon her.

"Isis! Osiris!" A thin, wavering voice, like a strand of fog, called out from the darkness. And then someone was helping her up, and two rather small dogs, who looked like fawns, were dancing around her feet.

"I do apologize," the voice said. "I hope you will forgive them. They don't see strangers often."

Gail took a long breath and opened her eyes. A very tall, very thin man, with a long narrow face, stood in front of her. There was something wrong with the face; one side was pulled down almost in a grimace, the eye pulled down, the corner of the mouth pulled down, so that the face seemed to have parts of two different faces. The man was wearing a very old leather jacket with a sheepskin collar and lining, a pair of faded chinos, and cracked leather bedroom slippers. He carried a lantern.

"Please do come in," he said, in that strange ghostly voice, "out of this beastly wind."

Gail was too frightened to move. "I'm . . . no, thank you," she said. "I was just looking for my cat."

"He's inside. I'm afraid my dogs alarmed him. But he's quite safe. They wouldn't hurt him. Down, Isis!" He raised a vague hand towards one of the dogs, and they both came to lean against his legs.

"If you wish to come in," he said, "we will find your cat. My mother said she thought he went up to the ballroom. She has remarkably acute hearing, my mother."

The presence of a mother seemed reassuring. "All right," Gail said. She followed the wavery figure to the door. As far as she could see, there was no light. But then he opened the door, and she saw the pale light of a kerosene lamp on a long trestle table.

The room was a gigantic kitchen. There was a black stove, a kitchen sink, and a cupboard that covered almost one whole wall. On the right there was a fireplace, and off in the far corner a big four-poster that seemed to be empty. A Boston rocker and a couch filled up the bay window; the pots of geraniums on the windowsill were a bright flare of color.

Gail hesitated in the doorway. She didn't see any signs of his mother, and she wasn't going further till she knew what she was getting into.

The dogs sat down in front of her and looked at her. They were fawn colored with tiny streaks of black in the undercoat. Their big alert ears were turned toward her, and their bright dark eyes examined her thoroughly. She noticed that their tails curled like a pig's. In spite of her dilemma, curiosity overcame her. "What kind of dogs are those?"

"Basenjis. A very ancient breed. They are descended from *lupus lupus*, rather than *canis lupus*. Very interesting breed."

"Oh," Gail said, not having any idea what he meant. *Lupus?*

"You may have seen them on engravings of old Egyptian tombs," the man said. "They have some of the characteristics of cats. For example, they wash themselves as a cat does; they climb trees, et cetera."

"Climb trees?" She looked at him suspiciously. He must think she was some kind of nut, to believe a dog climbed trees.

"Yes. And they don't bark. Although they *can* bark if they choose to. I once heard

Osiris here let out with a real bark when he was startled. Do come in!"

She realized that the wind from the open doorway was blowing everything around. She would either have to come in or go away. Go away into the cold darkness, without Sylvester. She stepped inside, and the man closed the door.

"Thank you," he said. "You must be very cold." One side of his face seemed to be smiling a little, but the other side remained rigid. Gail tried not to look at him.

"No, I'm fine," she said.

"Give her a cup of tea."

Gail jumped. It was a high small voice, and she had no idea where it came from. For one wild instant she reverted to her childhood belief in ghosts. A disembodied voice had to be a ghost. She seized the latch of the door.

Then, as the man moved toward the big stove, a small shape sat up in the bed. It was a very old woman, so tiny that her body had made no noticeable mound in the enormous four-poster. Her white hair was combed flat against her head and caught in a knot in the back. She looked at Gail with piercing black eyes.

"I don't believe I've met this young person, Sonny," the old woman said. Even in the shadows her eyes sparkled with merriment, and Gail had the feeling that the woman was on the edge of laughter.

"Excuse me, Mother," the man said, in his eerie voice. "This is the young lady who belongs to the cat."

"What is your name?" the old woman said.

"Gail," she said, wishing at once that she hadn't. As soon as they knew her name, they would call the authorities and Uncle Chad would come and get her. But she saw no telephone anywhere, and they didn't ask what her last name was.

"I am Mrs. Partridge. This is Sonny, my oldest boy. Where are the other children, Sonny?" She looked around the shadowy room.

"They're gone, Mother." He said it as if he had said it many times before, gently and patiently. He was setting out three teacups on the long wooden table.

Gail tried to take in as much of the big room as she could. It looked as if Mrs. Partridge and her son did most of their living in this one room. She wondered if they might be caretakers. But who would hire such an ancient woman and such a strange-looking man? She wondered where Sylvester was.

"I think my cat came in here," she said.

"Yes. The dogs chased him upstairs." Mrs.

Partridge leaned over and patted one of the basenjis. He looked up at her, wrinkling his forehead. He had beautiful eyes with a narrow black stripe, like eye-liner, that outlined the oval of his eyes. "After you've had a cup of tea, Sonny will take you to find him. He's a handsome cat."

Gail felt a little better about the old woman. If she had sense enough to admire Sylvester — "He's a nice cat," she said. But she knew better than to trust strangers; or anybody else, for that matter, except perhaps Miss Blake.

Sonny came over and helped his mother out of bed. "We were just going to have tea," he said to Gail.

Standing up, Mrs. Partridge looked even smaller than she had in bed. She reminded Gail of a baby bird she had once held in the palm of her hand, all fragile bones and soft feathers with bright eyes. What puzzled Gail was that, except for asking her name, they had asked no questions. It would be only natural to want to know who she was and where she came from, falling into their garden in a snowstorm the way she had. Whatever their reasons were for not asking, she was glad; it would give her time to think of some tricky answers.

Sonny poured the tea into the beautiful little china cups. Thick cream filled a cut-glass pitcher, and there were sugar cubes with tiny, colored rosebuds on them. The spoons were coin silver, which Gail recognized because she had a half-dozen that her grandmother had left her. It occurred to her that she should have brought them with her; that awful social worker would probably steal them.

She and Mrs. Partridge sat down as Sonny opened the door of the big black stove and took out a plateful of blueberry muffins. When he passed them, Gail realized she was hungry.

"These are wonderful," she said, remembering not to talk with her mouth full. Her mother was always after her about that.

"Sonny is a very good cook," Mrs. Partridge said. "Of course, this year's berries aren't ripe yet, but he had some jars still left in the cellar." She buttered a muffin delicately and popped a piece into her mouth. "All my children are good cooks."

"How many children do you have?" Gail asked politely. She had to talk about something, and the woman had brought up the subject of her children twice.

For a moment, Mrs. Partridge looked confused, and Sonny quickly said, "Five." He nodded at Gail. "All of them gone but me."

Gail didn't know whether "gone" meant dead or moved away, and she decided not to ask. She hated being questioned herself.

"Have another muffin, child," Mrs. Partridge said, pulling herself back from some momentary dream. "A growing child needs good nourishing food." She patted her silky white hair. "Did the hostiles bother you?"

"Hostiles?"

"The Indians don't bother people nowadays, Mother," Sonny said. He looked at Gail with his one-sided smile. "And I suppose the truth of it is, they never would have if white men had left them alone."

"They kidnapped my little sister," Mrs. Partridge said. "I call that bothering."

Gail glanced uneasily into the shadows behind her. Was she going to have to worry about Indians, too? But that kind of thing didn't happen anymore, did it? And Mrs Partridge had said "my little sister." It must have happened a million years ago when Mrs. Partridge was a girl. She looked at her, trying to imagine her as a little girl, all those years ago when Indians were "hostiles." Here, in this kitchen, in the soft circle of light made by the kerosene lamp, with the shadows at their backs and no sign anywhere of modern conveniences, Gail almost felt as if she were falling into some faraway time herself. She sat up straighter and blinked her eyes. She was tired out and getting silly.

"You must be very tired," Mrs. Partridge said, "after your long journey. Sonny, help the child find her cat. Then, why don't you fix up Robert's room for her? Better hang the blanket on a chair by the stove; it's bound to be cold. Sheets, too. I think the Hudson's Bay blanket would be best."

The notion of sleeping in this peculiar house, with strangers, jolted Gail awake. "I don't want to be a bother. If you could just give me directions to the nearest motel. . . ."

"Nonsense! No bother at all." Mrs. Partridge stood up, looked for her walking stick, and, like a slightly drunken ballerina, staggered back to the huge bed.

Sleepily, Gail watched Sonny leave the room, and come back a few minutes later with the colorfully striped Hudson's Bay blanket and some white sheets, which he spread over chairbacks near the stove. He lit a small hand lamp, and said, "Shall we look for your cat?"

It wasn't until they started out of the kitchen that Gail wondered how Mrs. Partridge knew she had come on a long journey.

7

GAIL STAYED SEVERAL SAFE STEPS behind
Sonny, although he kept lifting the lamp and
waiting for her so she could see. If he tried
anything creepy, she already had her plan of
action worked out: She would kick him hard
in the shins, punch him in the stomach, and
run. He was so tall and skinny, he shouldn't
be hard to handle, and she'd noticed that he
dragged one foot a little and seemed to have
trouble with the arm on that same side. He
wouldn't be nearly as strong as Uncle Chad.

From the kitchen they went into a room
that was considerably smaller, with floor-to-
ceiling cupboards that had leaded glass
doors. There were shelves, too, and a sink in
one corner. A cot, neatly made, was pulled
close to the outside wall, and there was an
old rolltop desk with what had to be the old-

est typewriter in the world sitting on it. Gail knew about typewriters because her mother was a secretary — a good one, too — and she was very temperamental about the kind of typewriter she had. The very latest IBM Selectric or nothing, that was what she always said. "Man!" Gail thought, "she should see this monstrosity!" A neatly stacked pile of manuscript pages lay beside the typewriter, with a rock on top of them to hold them down. It was a pretty rock with red streaks in it.

"Who lives here?" Gail asked.

He looked at her. She had noticed that he took a moment before he answered anything. She wondered if that was suspicious. Sometimes she did that, when she wanted to think up a plausible story.

"I do," he said. "This used to be the pantry, but now it's my little house."

What did you make of a man who lived in a pantry and called it his little house, and wrote something or other on the oldest typewriter in the world? Either they were crazies or they were running some kind of illegal operation.

Warning her of the threshold, he took her into a long hall that smelled of mildew. Gail jumped as they passed what looked — in the dark — like an enormous cavern with white shapes in its shadows.

As if he sensed her alarm, he said, "It looks ghostly, doesn't it? Mother keeps sheets over the furniture. I've never quite understood the logic of it."

When they reached the end of the hall, they started up a broad staircase with a white banister. The polished wood of the steps gleamed in the lamplight. And on the wall were a pair of candle sconces, without candles now, the many small pieces of glass in their reflectors throwing off patterns of light as the glow from Sonny's lamp caught them. A millionaire must have lived here, Gail thought, and maybe these people murdered him so they could have the house; only now they were too old and beat-up to run the whole thing, so they lived in the kitchen. Ahead of her, on the wall at the top of the stairs, Sonny's shadow danced, enormously long and distorted. She shivered.

"Sylvester's probably too scared to come out," she said, more loudly than she meant to. "Here, Sylvester, here, boy!" She whistled. People always laughed at her for whistling up a cat, but Sylvester knew what it meant. She felt an urgent need to hold Sylvester in her arms. Maybe he was dead; maybe those dogs had torn him to pieces. But she couldn't imagine, even in this dark and scary place, anything happening to Sylvester because of those pretty little dogs. He could handle both of them with one paw tied behind his back, even if they did get mean, which seemed unlikely when you remembered their eyes.

"He may be in the ballroom," Sonny said.

"Ballroom?" He had to be putting her on. People didn't have ballrooms.

He looked back at her and smiled his half-smile. "It seems odd, doesn't it? People don't live that way any more. But when my grandfather built this house, they did things up in style."

Grandfather. Well, she wasn't ready to buy that. "He must have been a billionaire, your grandfather," she said, with a touch of mockery to let him know she wasn't being had, "to build a house like this just to live in."

"He was an ostentatious man." He stood back to let her go through a pair of double doors.

At first she couldn't see where she was at all, and she tensed, ready for a showdown. But then he followed her, holding up the lamp. She gasped. They were in a room almost as big as her school auditorium. At one end of the room was the biggest piano she had ever seen. Along the walls there was a frieze of figures that looked like some she had seen in pictures of Greek temples. Overhead six huge crystal chandeliers reflected the light of the lamp. The main part of the floor was covered with a canvas, but around the edges the wood gleamed as if it had just been polished.

"Wow!" she said.

Sonny was looking around the room with a faraway expression. "Sometimes I can see them . . ." he said, so quietly she almost didn't hear him. "My grandfather always gave a ball for the incoming governor, regardless of his party affiliation. That is, after we became a state, of course, which was not until 1889. Before that, the guest of honor would always be the territorial official. He once gave a ball for the entire Tivoli Opera Company. They came in their stagecoaches, over the muddy roads. And others . . . Mrs. Pat Campbell, Lillian Russell, Grace George, the Barrymores, Minnie Maddern Fiske, Modjeska, Lotta Crabtree. . . . They have all danced here, shedding the radiance of their talent like the brilliance of the northern lights. . . ." He broke off suddenly, as if he had just remembered she was there. "Have you ever heard of any of those people?"

"I've heard of the Barrymores." She didn't add that she did not believe for a minute that any Barrymores had danced in this room, in this godforsaken wilderness. The man was plainly crazy.

"I think your cat must be in one of the bedrooms," he said. "He doesn't seem to be here. If he was really frightened by the dogs, he may have gone up into one of the cupolas."

Gail went out into the hall and whistled for Sylvester. She wasn't going up into any darned cupola in the dark. "Sylvester! Here, Syl, here, Syl!"

And there he was bounding down the stairs from the third floor and flying into her arms with such enthusiasm he almost knocked her over. She felt so relieved, she thought she was going to cry. She rubbed her face against his, listening to his lovely, familiar purr that her mother said sounded like sandpaper on rough wood. "Sylvester, where've you been? You scared me half to death."

8

BEFORE SHE BLEW OUT the lamp, she looked around once more at the little room Sonny had given her. He had apologized for its smallness, then smiled and said, "But you are a small person." It had been part of the servants' quarters, and he had given her this room because it opened onto the kitchen and would be warmer. "Our nights turn cold." She knew that already.

Next to her room there was a weird bathroom with a huge bathtub that sat up off the floor on feet that looked like lion's claws. The faucets looked like golden dragons and only the cold water faucet worked, but Sonny had brought her a big basin of hot water.

She lay back on her pillow, after she had blown out the lamp and Sylvester had settled himself across her feet. A fire burned low in a small, deeply recessed fireplace. A rise of the land outside her room had necessitated putting the windows up high, almost to the ceiling. There was a pole with a hook on it that you could open them with, but after she opened one, she closed it again — all but a crack — because of the cold wind that whistled outside.

Mrs. Partridge had given her a flannel nightgown, but she didn't want to put it on. Instead, she wore her underwear and pulled the wool blanket up around her neck.

"Wow, what a crazy situation to be in," she said to Sylvester. His golden eyes gleamed sleepily in the firelight.

She had fastened the big iron bolt on the door, but she still lay awake, feeling uneasy. Even if these people were just harmless old crazies, who still thought it was 1880 or something, you never knew what harmless old crazies would take it into their heads to do. Like talk to the sheriff. She had her twenty-three dollars but no clothes or anything, except what she was wearing. Uncle Chad would be looking for her as soon as he could stagger out of bed; she was darned sure of that. He probably had the cops out already. He wouldn't be about to let a free slave slip out of his hands that easy.

She dozed, then started awake when a log in the fireplace crackled. With all those open fires and kerosene lamps, it was a wonder the house didn't burn down. But it never had, and it had been there a long, long time

She tried to imagine all the people who might have slept in the bed in which she lay and have stared up at the patterns the fire made on the ceiling, the way she was doing now. It gave her the shivers. They hadn't even known it was weird to have a bathtub with lion's claws and no electricity anywhere, not even a flashlight. She wished she was back in that faraway time though, because then Uncle Chad wouldn't even have been born.

At last she fell asleep.

9

SHE AWOKE with a jerk to find a pattern of sunshine slanting down from the east window onto her bed. She sat up, clutching her blanket around her. The fire had gone out, and the room was chilly. The man had told her she could leave her door partly open, to get some of the heat from the kitchen, but she hadn't been about to do that.

"Good morning," she said to Sylvester. It would be nice to be a cat. You'd always have a nice fur coat that just needed a little washing, now and then; and you could find mice and things for dinner if you had to.

Food. She sniffed. Somebody was frying bacon, and she was hungry. Maybe she could buy her breakfast from these people and then look around for some way to get out of here. She got dressed quickly and washed up in cold water.

"Good morning," the man said, when she

cautiously pushed open the door into the kitchen. "I hope you slept well." In the daylight he looked even taller, skinnier, and stranger than he had before. He had on old faded chinos that had shrunk, so they didn't even reach his ankles, and a black-and-white-checked wool shirt. He was frying bacon.

"Fine, thank you." Gail looked around the room. Where was the old lady? She frowned suspiciously. Maybe she wasn't so old and helpless as she looked. Maybe she'd gone to tell the neighbors about Gail.

The kitchen door opened and Mrs. Partridge came in, leaning on her cane and carrying a basketful of eggs. She nodded brightly at Gail. "Morning. Beautiful morning. Spring decided to come back." She put the eggs down carefully on the kitchen table. "That Rhode Island Red is laying just fine."

"I thought she would," Sonny said. "She had a cooperative look about her." He broke the eggs into a bowl. He smiled at Gail. "Do you like omelets?"

"Omelets?" She tried to remember what an omelet was. Her mother or she herself usually tossed eggs into the frying pan and they were done when she remembered to take them out. "Yes, sure." A hen that looked cooperative? These people were really gone in the head.

All through breakfast Mrs. Partridge talked about her hens. She and her son discussed how many chickens they should get this year.

"Get a lot," Mrs. Partridge said. "I love to hear 'em chirping away there, under the stove."

Under the stove? Gail stared at the big iron stove and tried to picture chickens underneath it. Impossible! There wouldn't be room for even one hen.

"Christopher likes a lot of chickens," Mrs. Partridge said. She passed the plate of hot buttered toast to Gail. "Eat up, child. You're a growing girl."

Gail took another piece of toast and wanted to ask who Christopher was, but she thought better of it. He'd probably turn out to be the rooster, and then she'd feel like a dope for having asked. "I'd like to pay for my breakfast," she said, instead. "How much do you charge?"

They both looked at her with such shocked surprise that she added quickly, "I mean, you don't even know me."

"We know you now," Mr. Sonny said. "You are our guest and we are honored to have you."

"Stay a long time, do," Mrs. Partridge said. "We'll fatten you up a little. Sonny's good cooking will do it. A growing child needs a little fat on her."

Gail didn't know what to think. Why should they want her to stay? In spite of what they said, she was a total stranger. For all they knew, she could be a drug addict or a thief or something. She peered at them out of the corner of her eyes as she ate. What were they up to? Maybe they thought there'd be a reward.

Maybe there was. It would be just like Uncle Chad to think of offering a reward, the way they used to do for runaway slaves. If he did that, everybody in the town would be fighting over who was going to catch her and turn her in. She'd have to make plans fast — right away.

She excused herself and went outside. In the daylight things looked different. The scary shapes of the night before were only trees and bushes, overgrown and untrimmed. At the far end of the path she had come down, she could see the faint white gleam of the marble Cupid.

Most of the snow was gone, leaving the barnyard muddy. More than a dozen hens and a big rooster wandered around, pecking at the ground. On a long, weatherbeaten picnic table, plates of chicken feed were set out, as if for a banquet of fowls. Now and then, a hen flapped up to the table and ate.

Sylvester lay stretched out on the lower limb of a willow tree, watching the hens with curiosity and caution. The two basenjis were playing, chasing each other in wide circles, making flying leaps over the chopping block, the woodpile, or sometimes the hens, who squawked indignantly each time. She had never seen dogs run like that, with so much speed and grace, as if they were almost floating. She called them, and they came to her at once, heads cocked on one side, mouths open, panting.

"I don't have anything for you. I just wanted to tell you, you're beautiful." She put her hand on Osiris' smooth head. Isis leaned against her knee. She patted them and straightened up. "You guys go play now. I've got to think."

She went down the path to the barn. She wanted to think where nobody could see her. She had the feeling around this family that they could see inside her head.

Although it was warm outside, the barn was cool and dusky. There were no animals in it, but there was an old high coach, like stagecoaches she had seen on TV, and there were lots of stalls. Underneath the haymow, where a little hay was strewn on the floor boards, a new-looking ten-speed bicycle leaned against the wall. Whose could that be? She tried to picture either of the Partridges on it but it was difficult. Possibly Mr. Sonny, only he was so tippy, it seemed as if he'd be sure to fall off. She ran her hand along the blue enameled metal. It was a nice bike.

The place smelled of hay and animals, and at first it made her wrinkle her nose, but then she decided she liked it. Once her mother had taken her to a place called The Barnyard, outside the city, where kids could pay a dime and look at farm animals, ducks and hens and things. She'd liked it, but they had never gone back.

She climbed up into the seat of the tall coach. It creaked. What would it have been like to come here in a contraption like this, instead of Uncle Chad's rented car? It would take forever. She jounced a little and the springs squeaked. "Giddap," she said softly.

But she couldn't just sit up there and daydream. She had to think what to do next. The cops were likely to come screaming up at any minute, and if they asked the Partridges if they'd seen her, naturally they'd say yes, she's right out there in the yard, somewhere.

And maybe they'd get a nice reward. They looked like people who could use it.

Maybe the cops would put her in jail till Uncle Chad got out of the hospital, if that's where he was. They wouldn't call it jail; they'd call it detention. She knew kids who had been in detention. It was jail, pure and simple.

She shivered. At the door of the barn, she peered out to see if anybody was looking. No one was in sight. For a minute she watched the thin column of smoke that drifted upward from the kitchen chimney. Quietly she called Sylvester, scooped him up in her arms, and ran around to the back of the house. From the hollow that the house was in, the land in back sloped down still further into woods. She ran down a path until she was in thick trees. The path led to a creek that raced along noisily, overflowing its banks with snow water.

She looked back at the house. It was silent and without any sign, except for the smoke, that anyone even lived there. She put Sylvester down and sat on a log near the creek. She was afraid to go any further into the woods; they were dark and she knew she'd get lost.

Sylvester climbed a birch tree and swung on a branch till he dropped off. He went up and did it again. She laughed. It reminded her of a poem she'd liked in school, about birch trees that the ice bends down so they look as if boys had swung on them. Or cats, she thought. She looked at a chipmunk who was watching her from the opposite bank. The woods might be a nice place to stay if you knew anything about them.

But she didn't. And she'd never have the nerve to stay out there at night. She'd just stay till it began to get dark, then sneak back to the house and see if the coast was clear.

She stretched out on her stomach on the log, but the bark was scratchy on her arms so she sat up again. It was going to be pretty boring to sit there all day.

10

IT WAS LATE AFTERNOON when she left the woods and climbed the slope to the house. She was tired and hungry and discouraged. Although she had walked a little way along the creek, she had been too uneasy in the unfamiliar gloom of the forest to go very far. Sylvester seemed to like it there, but she found herself jumping at every little sound. And getting more and more bored. She had played word games; she had drawn a tic-tac-toe diagram in the dirt with a stick and competed against herself; she had told herself wild, fantastic stories about taking a trip into outer space and settling down on a nice, friendly planet, where everything sparkled and was clean and there were wonderful things to eat. But, finally, she had run clear out of things to think about, except Uncle

Chad and what he would do to her. He would be so mad when he found her, he'd really beat up on her.

She approached the house cautiously. As far as she could tell, there were no tire tracks in the yard. There were footprints, a man's, but they could be Mr. Sonny's. Some of them led to his vegetable garden, where he had some plants growing inside a glass frame, and a couple of rows of white paper caps stuck into the ground. Some of the other prints went on toward the road, but maybe he'd just gone out for a walk or to a mailbox or something.

She pushed open the kitchen door and went inside. He looked up from the long table, where he sat reading a book. The old lady was asleep in her big bed.

He smiled at her. "Did you have a nice day?"

Not a question. Not a word about where she had been and why she had disappeared. It made her suspicious. She wasn't used to people who didn't ask questions.

"I was just looking around. At the . . . uh . . ." Gail should have thought out what she was going to say; that was a bad slip. "At the trees and things."

He nodded, as if that were perfectly normal. "If you want to go out tomorrow, I'll fix you a sandwich. You must be hungry."

"Oh, I hadn't thought about it." She hoped her stomach wouldn't rumble. "Anyway, I'll have to be moving on pretty soon. I've got to meet my father. . . . He's been delayed. . . ." She'd always thought of herself as an expert liar; but with Mr. Sonny sitting there looking at her, she knew she was doing a terrible job. "Nobody came with any message for me, I suppose?"

"No." He looked at her for a moment and then got up. "I'm roasting a leg of lamb but it isn't quite finished. Why don't I fix you a little sandwich to tide you over?"

She started to say, "I don't need it," but hunger overcame her. She stood watching in almost desperate impatience as his slow, shaky hands put together a sliced cheese-and-tomato sandwich.

"There," he said. "That should help."

She thanked him and sat down at the table, trying not to wolf down the sandwich. He poured a glass of milk for her, then sat down again with his book.

"You'll excuse me if I go on reading. I'm in a very exciting chapter." He smiled again.

"Sure. Of course." She was relieved that he didn't want to talk. Talking was too dangerous. She tried to read the title of the book but his long fingers covered the words.

He glanced up. *"Moby Dick,"* he said. "I guess I must have read it a dozen times, but I still find it very exciting."

"Oh." There he goes again, she thought, reading my mind. She finished her sandwich and her milk and went into her own room. She lay down on the comfortable bed and tried to think, but instead she fell asleep.

When Mr. Sonny knocked gently on her door to tell her dinner was ready, she leaped up in terror. But there was no cop, no sheriff, no Uncle Chad. Only a marvelous dinner, and Mrs. Partridge chattering away about one time when she'd been to San Francisco. "Just a week before the fire," she said. Gail stared at her in disbelief. Everybody knew the San Francisco fire was about a thousand years ago. Who was she kidding?

The next day, when Gail left again for the forest, she found a package of sandwiches left for her by Mr. Sonny, whom she could see working away in his garden. This time she took a book that she had found in her room, a very old-looking copy of Dickens's *Bleak House.* She was not, as a rule, much of a reader; there was always too much that had to be done at home. But, sitting with her back propped against a pine tree and the chatter of the creek in her ears, she became absorbed in the problems of Ada and Esther. If those kids could get out of the messes they were in, maybe she could get out of hers. She was not surprised to find that court orders had loused up everybody's lives, even way back then.

When she went back to the house, in the late afternoon, she was startled back to the reality of her own problem by the clear tracks of tires in the yard. Somebody had come in, in a car. She thought of hiding out in the barn for a while, where she could keep an eye on things, but just then Mr. Sonny came dragging up the path from his garden.

As he had done yesterday, he nodded pleasantly, as if everything were perfectly normal. "Time to fix dinner," he said, and opened the door for her.

Again, dinner was as casual as if Gail were an old friend who had dropped in for a visit. Nobody mentioned the tire tracks in the yard, and she couldn't think of any way to ask about them without arousing suspicion.

It was beginning to get on her nerves, not knowing what Uncle Chad was up to. If he were looking for her, or if he had the cops looking for her, it wouldn't make sense for them not to inquire at the Partridges. It was the only house she had seen in the area near where the accident had happened. Maybe Uncle Chad was dead! She felt guilty at the wave of relief that swept over her as she considered that possibility. It wasn't right to wish somebody dead, especially a relative. But it *would* make things a whole lot simpler. She wished the Partridges got a newspaper so she could check. But there was no sign of one.

She went to bed early and read some more of *Bleak House*, but indoors it was harder to keep her mind on the book. She found herself listening hard for any unusual noises. Sometimes the woodwork cracked, or somewhere off in the big house something creaked. Each time she was instantly alert, listening, ready to run.

In the morning it was raining and the wind was blowing. She didn't know what to do. She couldn't go sit in the woods all day in the pouring rain, but she felt trapped in the house. Mr. Sonny lit a fire for her in the library. It was a dark room, with heavy draperies. The book-lined walls and the big dark-blue oriental rug were nice, though.

She opened the draperies at the window that faced the yard, so she could spot a car if one drove up. With all the racket the wind and rain were making, she might not hear it. She sat down on an ottoman in front of the fireplace and sighed. It would be nice if she could relax; she could really enjoy this room, with the fire and all, if she didn't have to be looking out for danger all the time.

She looked at the small, elegant desk in the corner of the room. It had a neat brown blotter in brown-leather corners, and there was a pad of paper and envelopes in the cubbyholes, and a couple of fountain pens. Suddenly, it occurred to her what she must do. It seemed so obvious, she couldn't understand why she hadn't thought of it before. She would write a letter to her father to come and get her. She'd already told the Partridges he was coming, but she'd said that as a lie. Why not make it come true? He always said to let him know if she needed him, and she would never need him any more than she did now.

She sat down at the desk and tore off a piece of paper. "Dear Dad," she wrote. "Mom is in the hospital again, real bad. Uncle Chad came to get me, but I got away from him. He's a very mean man and I'm not going to go with him. He's in the hospital here, I think. We had a car crash. But I know he'll get the cops after me. I'm hiding out with some people named Partridge, but I don't know if they can be trusted. Please come quick. Very quick, please! I'll draw you a map of where I am." She turned the paper over and drew a map of where she was, as nearly as she could remember it in relation to the town and the road.

Now the question was: how to mail the letter? First of all, she needed an airmail stamp. She noticed a little leather box on the desk, about the size of a stamp box. She felt guilty about touching it, but she did need a stamp desperately. It was practically a matter of life and death. She looked back quickly at the door, then opened the box. It had a one-cent stamp and three eights. No airmail. But she could use two eights. She took them out and put them on the envelope. Then she got a quarter out of her pocket and put it in the box. That more than paid for it.

Second question: how to get the letter mailed? She couldn't go into town, herself, and Mr. Sonny never seemed to leave the place. There must be someplace where he got his mail, though; a box out on the road? She'd seen those footprints. She'd look in the morning. The letter ought to be mailed right away because it would take several days to get to Hawaii. And he might not even be there. What if he hadn't left a forwarding address? She put the thought out of her mind, and settled down by the fireplace to read some more of *Bleak House*. The book was full of scary people, and every now and then she jumped and looked over her shoulder when a board creaked somewhere in the house.

11

THAT NIGHT, after dinner, Mrs. Partridge taught her to play gin rummy. She didn't want to play; she was never any good at card games. But she couldn't think of any polite reason to refuse. After she caught on to it, she began to enjoy it. Mrs. Partridge played with a great deal of enthusiasm, and when she won, she'd throw her hands up in the air and shout, "Gin!" In spite of herself, Gail found herself laughing. For such an old lady, Mrs. Partridge was very peppy.

Mr. Sonny sat reading his book, and every now and then he looked at them over his glasses and smiled.

When she went to bed, the wind was really howling. She lay huddled up in the blanket, listening to a thumping noise somewhere outside her room. She couldn't tell what it was and it scared her. She listened to the dull, irregular thumps. They seemed to be just outside her window, as if something were trying to get in. Her heart raced. Sylvester sat up and stared hard at the high window. Gail's terror grew. Something or someone was out there.

Finally, she decided she had to find out what it was, no matter what. She got out of bed, pulled a chair up to the window, and looked out. She almost fell backward off the chair as a black shape threw itself across the window. Then she caught the sill and went limp with relief. The wind was blowing the branch of a tree against the window.

She tumbled back into bed. Afraid of the wind! She could imagine how her mother would tease her about that. Thinking of her mother made her feel so sad, she tried to find something else to think about. Miss Blake. If only there were a phone in this place, she could call up Miss Blake. Only what could Miss Blake do for her? Nothing. As long as Uncle Chad had that court order, they were all helpless, except perhaps her father. He never paid any attention to court orders; at least, he'd never paid any attention to the one about alimony. She went to sleep at last.

A faint tinge of light in the eastern sky had just reached her windows when a noise awoke her. It wasn't the branch this time. She could hear rain, but the wind seemed to have gone down. Someone was trying to get her window open. With a gasp she sat up. Before she could think, the window opened, and a tall form scrambled in and leaped into the middle of the room. Gail fell out of bed.

For a moment there was absolute stillness. Gail lay on the floor, half wrapped in the blanket that she had dragged off when she fell, too paralyzed with fear even to breathe. Sylvester had leaped up to the windowsill and sat staring down at her. The tall dark shape that had sprung into the room hadn't moved. Gail got up the courage to look at him. It was hard to see him in the shadowy gray light, but she saw that it was not Sonny or Uncle Chad or anyone she had ever seen before. Her first thought was that it was a policeman sent by Uncle Chad to get her. She was not going without a fight.

Still hanging onto the blanket, she got to her feet. "I've got a gun," she said. "You think I'm kidding but it's true. It's a gun with six bullets . . . and if you take one step toward me, I'll shoot you dead six times. I mean it!"

"Once would be more than enough." He had a nice voice, but she'd known a detective who had a nice voice too.

She narrowed her eyes, trying to make out

what this one looked like. He seemed young to be a cop, not more than eighteen or so, but maybe they hired them young in the country. "What do you want?"

He put his hands on his hips. His hair came to the collar of his nylon parka and his boots were muddy. "Who are you?" he asked.

"I happen to be the house guest of the Partridges."

He snorted. "They don't have house guests."

"Well, they've got one now."

"Listen, kid, I don't know what you're up to, but you better get yourself together and buzz on out of here. I don't want any trouble."

"Trouble for who?"

"For the Partridges. Who do you think?"

She was confused. He wasn't saying the right things. "I could turn you in for breaking in on me like that," she said, trying a new tack. "You've got no search warrant."

"I don't need a search warrant to enter my own house."

"Oh, sure," she said, "it's your house, and you're Mr. Sonny's great-grandfather, and you always come into the house flying through a window like Peter Pan."

He stared down at her for a moment. Then

he went to the door that led to the hall. He unbolted it. "I see you locked the door against the ghosts. Good thinking." He went out into the hall, closing the door behind him. The room smelled faintly of fish.

"Smart guy," she muttered, but she was puzzled. It couldn't be true that he lived here; she'd seen most of the house, except the third floor and the cupolas, and there was no sign of anybody living anywhere but in the kitchen and Sonny's pantry. She wondered if she ought to wake Sonny in case this was a burglar. She decided to keep an eye out. She dressed quickly and let herself into the big, dark hall. If she stayed where she could watch the stairs, she'd see him if he were trying to make a heist.

She chose a spot just inside the door of the library, where she could see the stairs and the front door. If he'd gone upstairs, or into the big living room or the dining room or the other room that looked like a parlor or something, then she'd see him. If there were any backstairs that she didn't know about, he might get away. The only alternative she could think of was to wake Mr. Sonny, and she was too scared to do that.

She made Sylvester sit in her lap, although he wanted to prowl around the room. She sat very still, almost holding her breath. She couldn't hear a sound. Deciding she needed a weapon, she got a poker from the fireplace. The intruder had been skinny and kind of tall, but if she took him by surprise, she could knock him out. She looked at the poker. It was pretty, with a round brass handle.

As the early light began to filter through the heavy draperies, she could see better. She moved to the big table in the middle of the room; it had two chairs like the one at the desk, with rose-colored velvet seats. She studied the big oil painting over the fireplace. It was a man on a horse. He looked a little like Mr. Sonny, except that he had on old-fashioned riding clothes. Maybe he was Sonny's father or grandfather or something. Mama had a picture of her grandmother, but it was the small kind that sits on a table. Gail had never thought much about it, except that the woman's hair looked so funny.

She stared at the portrait for several minutes and then looked at the desk, wondering if the man in the painting had ever sat at the desk. She shivered. This was a spooky house; it got you all mixed up about what the real time was.

Although she stayed in the library a long while, she heard no sound and saw no one. At last there were breakfast smells from the direction of the kitchen. She went back to her room and let Sylvester out the high window. "Don't run away, now," she told him. She washed her face and brushed her teeth with a Kleenex. She wished she had her suitcase! She was tired of wearing the same clothes every day, even though she was now sleeping in the nightgown and washing out her underwear before she went to bed.

When she went into the kitchen, Sonny was standing at the stove, and Mrs. Partridge was at the table, peeling an orange. Sonny smiled, and Mrs. Partridge said, "Good morning, my dear. I hope you slept well. Breakfast is going to be lovely; Christopher brought us brook trout."

Gail swallowed. "Christopher?"

"She hasn't met Christopher yet, Mother," Sonny said. "Christopher is my nephew."

"My great-grandson," Mrs. Partridge said. "My own dear boy."

"Oh." Gail took the orange Mrs. Partridge offered her. "Uh . . . does he live here? Christopher, I mean."

"When he's home," Mrs. Partridge said. "He spends a lot of time in the woods."

"He's a naturalist," Sonny said.

"Oh. He doesn't look . . . I mean, is he very old?"

Sonny poured a cup of coffee for her. "He's

just graduated from high school, but he's always been a naturalist. He's quite gifted in that way. Kind of a young Thoreau."

All Gail remembered about Thoreau was that he had written some dull thing about a pond. But as she tasted the first bite of the pan-fried trout, she stopped thinking about Thoreau. "Wow! I never tasted anything this good."

Sonny beamed on the one side of his face that registered expression. "There's nothing as good as a fresh-caught fish."

"My father was a nature-loving man," Mrs. Partridge said. "Christopher favors the Lowell side."

The back door opened and Christopher came in, the two basenjis at his heels. Gail swallowed a mouthful of coffee and burned her throat. He was carrying the poker from the library, swinging it as if it were a walking stick.

"Good morning," he said. He kissed his great-grandmother's white hair and put his hand on Sonny's shoulder. "How are you?" He hadn't looked at Gail.

"Good morning, dear," his great-grandmother said. "It's good to see you. You look fine."

He had combed his long brown hair, and

this morning he wasn't wearing the nylon parka. Instead, he had on a blue-flannel shirt and jeans.

"This is Gail, dear, our house guest."

Gail shot him a look of triumph.

"Gail, this is our Christopher."

"How do you do," Gail said primly.

He nodded, without a glimmer of recognition. "Glad to meet you." He put the poker on the table.

"Whatever are you doing with that poker?" Mrs. Partridge said.

"Oh, I happened to notice it in the library. It was out of place. Thought I might as well polish it while I was about it." Without looking at Gail, he sat down at the table.

"Will you be home for long?" Sonny said, in his slow, thin voice.

"Not awfully. What needs doing?"

"I thought we'd better get the beans in. The frost is out of the ground."

"All right. Sure. Good thing we didn't have them in before that storm hit."

"Yes. I was glad I had the hot caps on the peas."

Christopher finished his coffee. "Somebody had an accident up on the road the night of the storm. Skidded into the ditch."

Gail stiffened, but he didn't look at her.

"I hope no one was hurt." Sonny looked concerned.

"The driver's in the hospital. Broke his arm and got a bad concussion, I heard. The car's a mess."

"Was anyone with him?"

Christopher shrugged. "Nobody seems to know. The guy's been out of his head, I guess, or unconscious or something. Henry Armitage found him in the wreck. Said somebody signaled him with a flashlight and then disappeared."

"Probably one of those hike-hitchers," Mrs. Partridge said.

Christopher smiled. "Could be, Gran."

"I've told you, I've told you all. No good can come of those machines. It's not a natural way to travel. God made the horse so man could travel."

Christopher reached over and squeezed her shoulder. "I'm with you, Gran."

Mrs. Partridge gazed intently into her glass of milk. "Covina died in her bed."

"That's all right, Mother," Sonny said gently.

Gail got up. "Excuse me. I'm going out for a minute."

She went to the barn and climbed up into

the coach again, hardly thinking about what she was doing. She was disturbed about what Christopher had said. If Uncle Chad had been unconscious, that was why nobody had tracked her down yet. But when he got better, and maybe he was already better, he'd be after her. She was disturbed that Christopher knew all about the accident. Without a doubt he had guessed that she was the one who had signaled with the flashlight. The question was, what would he do about it?

Just then he came outside, carrying a pan of corn for the hens. He put it in the dishes on the table, and the hens flapped up onto the table.

He saw her watching him. "Gran thinks hens ought to have a table to eat off of, like anybody else."

What was there to say to that? "That little hen isn't getting any."

"She will." He squinted his eyes at her. "You haven't ever heard of the pecking order?"

"What's that?"

He banged the dish to get the last kernels out. "You're from the city, I guess. Some city. Where are you from?"

"Who, me? I'm from ... uh ... Alaska." It

was the farthest-away place she could think of at the moment.

"Yeah? I used to live in Alaska."

"Oh, sure." If she'd said Timbuctoo, he'd have said he used to live there.

"Whereabouts in Alaska? Nome? Sitka? Anchorage?"

"Oh, all over."

"I spent ten years in Nome. My dad was a bush pilot."

She began to feel nervous. Maybe he really had lived in Alaska. "Why aren't you there now?"

"My parents were lost in their plane. They were flying supplies in to a fish-and-game guy. They disappeared." He said it matter-of-factly.

If it were true, it was terrible. But what could you believe? She remembered her vow to believe nothing. "That's too bad," she said, her voice as casual as his.

"Look," he said, "don't hang around here if it's going to make trouble for Gran and Uncle Sonny."

Startled, she said, "What do you mean?"

"I don't want them mixed up in anything." He reached into his jeans pocket and pulled out a twenty-dollar bill. He held it out to her.

"What's that?"

"Twenty bucks. Use it to get out of here."

"I don't need your money." She couldn't figure him out.

"Take it, anyway. If you're ever in the neighborhood, you can pay me back. If not, forget it."

"How do you know I don't live in the neighborhood?"

"Because you live in Alaska. Remember? Besides, I know everybody around here."

She was trying to think fast. "Do you know where there's a mailbox?"

It was his turn to look puzzled. "Mailbox?"

"I have to get a message to my father right away. He's supposed to meet me near here. But my plans got a little changed. I have to let him know where I am." It didn't sound too good. She could see he didn't believe it.

"There's one up at the end of the road, by the highway. I'll mail your letter for you."

"No. I'll do it. Thanks." She turned away. She didn't want to talk to him anymore. He made her nervous.

He went back to the house, and in a few minutes he came out again with a fishing rod and creel. He took the path that led past the barn to the woods. When he went past Gail, he said, "You be gone when I get back, okay?" He didn't wait for an answer.

She watched him stride off. "I'll go when I'm good and ready," she said, under her breath.

If he'd gone off fishing, maybe she wouldn't have him to worry about for a little while. She walked up the road to find the mailbox.

It made her uneasy to walk along the road. If somebody came around one of those curves in a hurry, she wouldn't have time to hide. But no one came. She stood in a clump of birches near the main road to be sure there were no cars in sight. Then she ran to the cluster of mailboxes and found the one that said Partridge. She put her letter inside.

One of the other boxes had its red metal flag up. She wasn't sure what it meant, but it seemed likely it was to tell the mailman there was a letter to be picked up, so she pulled up the flag on the Partridge box, too.

She heard a car coming up the road. She darted back into the trees and waited. It went on by; it was an old pickup. She ran down the road to the Partridge place and climbed the wall, as she had the night she came. She said "hi" to the marble Cupid.

For now, she had decided to sit tight and wait until she heard from her father. It was the only thing she could think of to do. And if anyone came looking for her, she would hide in one of the upper rooms in the house, maybe in one of those weird cupolas. The house was so big, it would be hard to find her, unless they brought a whole squad and a bunch of tear gas or something. Anyway it was the best she could do.

She picked up Sylvester. He didn't want to go inside, but she didn't trust that rooster. She'd heard of geese attacking people; for all she knew, a rooster might attack a cat. She stepped over the two dogs, who lay half asleep in the sunshine like figures in an Egyptian tomb. Not that she'd ever had much to do with Egyptian tombs. It was just that if you lived around the Partridges long enough, you got to thinking that way.

"Are you Isis or Osiris?" she said to one of the dogs. He looked up at her, the wrinkles in his forehead deepening as if he were thinking. She'd heard about Isis and Osiris in school, but she couldn't remember who they were, exactly. Some kind of gods.

Sylvester leaped out of her arms, and in an instant the two dogs and the cat were racing around the yard in a wild game of tag. Gail knew there was no sense in trying to catch Sylvester when he was acting kittenish, so she went into the kitchen.

Mrs. Partridge was sitting at the table, with a deck of strange-looking cards in front of her, which she was studying. She was wrapped up in a pink-flannel bathrobe that was too big for her. Gail noticed that her fleece-lined slippers were on the floor, her bare feet dangling above them. Mr. Sonny was sorting out what looked like weeds, tying them in little bunches.

He looked up and smiled his half-smile. "I'm tying up the early crop of herbs," he said. "We dry them. They smell so nice." He held out a green sprig. Cautiously, Gail sniffed. It did smell good.

"What is it?"

"Rosemary."

"That's for remembrance," Mrs. Partridge murmured, without looking up.

"What are those cards?" Gail didn't like to ask questions, but sometimes she just couldn't help it. They were really weird-looking cards, with pictures of knights and things on them.

"Tarot cards," Mr. Sonny said

"They foretell the future." Mrs. Partridge looked up, now all in the present.

"Tell the future! You don't believe in *that* stuff, do you?" Gail looked at Sonny.

He smiled. "Tarot goes far back in man's history, at least to the Egyptians. The first cards were painted on parchment, or sometimes on thin sheets of silver or gold or ivory."

"But telling the future," Gail said, "that's like putting a penny in the weight machine and it comes out, saying 'you'll travel across water and meet a handsome stranger.' Nobody believes that stuff."

"Man lives by symbols," Sonny said. "What we like to call magic is perhaps only the great sea of half-felt truth that man has always just dipped his toes into."

"Nobody believes in magic, after they're ten years old," Gail said. She had never heard a grown-up say magic was anything but nonsense. She peered at the cards that were spread out in front of Mrs. Partridge, strange-looking cards, one of a silly-looking boy or girl in a tunic, holding a cup with a fish sticking out of it; another of a hand holding a thing like an hourglass with a bird sticking his beak into a circle that had a cross; one of a whole bunch of sticks. There were nine cards laid out, four of them in a straight line, the rest in a kind of cross.

"What's that one mean?" Gail pointed to the boy or girl, whichever it was.

"That is you, dear," Mrs. Partridge said.

Gail was startled. "Me?"

"The Page of Cups represents a young person, unmarried, with light-brown hair and hazel eyes." She glanced up at Gail. "A young person with strong feelings, sometimes melancholy, but full of imagination. Touch the cards with the tips of your fingers, please, my dear. And think your question."

Feeling foolish, yet also beginning to feel a little prickle of fear that was almost pleasant, she touched the cards. Mrs. Partridge bent over them, her face wrinkled with concentration. She began to talk in a quick, low voice. Gail could hardly hear her at times.

"The Two of Cups here . . . the start of a warm friendship with someone of the opposite sex, a kindred soul. Here's the Eight of Wands . . . you have come through the countryside in great haste. There is a message to someone . . . the Six of Swords. . . ."

Mrs. Partridge paused. Gail stared down at the card. It showed a man poling a boat in which a woman sat, huddled up and dejected. Six swords stood up from the gunwales of the boat.

"The future will improve. You will be relieved of your anxiety. You will find . . . you will find a new home. You will gain new understanding. The Nine of Swords. . . ."

Gail shuddered at the picture of a woman

sitting up in bed, her hands to her head in an attitude of despair. The nine swords formed a wall behind her.

"Suffering, suffering . . . illness. . . ." Mrs. Partridge's voice grew faint, and Gail bent down to listen. "Misery." She was silent for a moment, her head bent down almost to the table. "Here is the Five of Swords, reversed. Possible defeat, sorrow . . . The Five of Pentacles."

"Why are these so gloomy?" Gail stared down at the ragged man on crutches, the woman in a shawl, walking in snow under a lighted window, never looking up at the light. She felt like crying.

Mrs. Partridge didn't hear her. "Loss of home. Lonely, lonely, a dark night of the spirit. . . ." Her voice trembled. Then it rose, almost with laughter in it. "But look! The Seven of Cups! Beautiful dreams! Castles in the air." Her voice lowered again. "But illusion, illusion."

"Can't you find anything good?" Gail said. She had forgotten Sonny, who stood very still at the stove. She had almost forgotten where she was. The cards drew her as if they were scenes from a play, a play about her.

"The Fool!" Mrs. Partridge's voice lifted again.

"A fool," Gail muttered. "That's all I need." But the young man in the picture looked carefree and happy. The sun shone on him and a little dog played at his feet.

"Inexperience, yes," Mrs. Partridge said, touching the card gently with her finger. "But he is the Power of Life. He faces the unknown but he laughs. Here, the wand he carries is the will, and in his purse he carries the memory of the race. He is strong — see here, the eagle. And the white rose . . . he is pure. Everything may be his — or nothing." The shadows cast by the kerosene lamp seemed to brighten and then dim. "But he has the choice. It is all any of us have. And here, at the last, the Ace of Cups."

Her voice seemed to grow stronger and younger, almost triumphant. "See the five streams of living water, the dove of peace, the sacred dew of spirit, the water lilies that speak of eternal life." She placed both hands flat over the cards. "A great joy begins here — Love. Great beauty and a mind filled with spirit." She sat very still, almost without breathing, for a long moment. Then she looked up at Gail for the first time and said matter-of-factly, "So you will be staying with us for a while, and I am so glad."

Gail felt drained. "How do you know that?"

"It's clear."

"I'm so pleased," Sonny said.

He sounded so genuinely happy that Gail looked at him quickly. "I don't think it will be all that long," she said. "My father will be coming for me."

Mrs. Partridge gathered up the cards, handling them gently; she folded a worn piece of silk around them and put them in a leather box. Sonny took the box and placed it on a shelf next to her bed.

"And now we need tea," Mrs. Partridge said.

"It's brewing, Mother." In a minute he poured it into three cups.

Gail thought of what Christopher had said about getting the Partridges into trouble. She wouldn't want that to happen. "I wish you'd let me pay you or something," she said, "till my father gets here."

"My child," Mr. Sonny said, "please don't think of such things."

"But you don't know anything about me. I could be real trouble. I could be a fugitive from justice or something."

"We pride ourselves on being good judges of character," Mrs. Partridge said. "And the cards have told me. This is your home for as long as you wish, to live in and to explore as you like. You are our welcome guest."

Gail flushed. She had been thinking of taking a look at the third floor, only she'd planned to do it in a sneaky way when they were asleep. This was one eerie old lady. "Thank you."

Mrs. Partridge bowed like a hostess at a tea. "At your pleasure." Suddenly, her head fell forward on her chest and she was sound asleep. Sonny picked her up and put her on the bed, covering her with a quilt.

"There," he said, "she'll sleep, probably well into the afternoon. The Tarot reading tires her."

Gail felt nervous. She felt as if she had been through some kind of emotional experience, but she wasn't sure whether it was good or bad.

12

THE NEXT DAY she was in her room when she heard a car. She climbed onto the chair to look out the window. It was an official car, with the state seal on the door. The man who got out wore a green uniform that had a patch on one sleeve. Sheriff! It had to be the sheriff.

She ran out of her room and up the staircase to the third floor. Now she was furious with herself for not having checked the upper floor for places to hide out. She had only thought about it, not done it. Now she'd have to trust to luck.

The third floor was smaller than the first two, and there was a narrow iron staircase that went up to still another level. Quickly she examined the rooms on the third floor. Some were empty, some had bedroom furniture; all were large, with big, walk-in closets. But closets would be the first place they'd

think to look for her. She tried the door of
one room, but it was stuck. Another closed
door led to a wing, but she decided not to
bother with that now.

She crouched near the top of the stairs and
listened. She could hear voices: Sonny's thin
slow voice and another one, deeper and
louder. The cop's! The voices came nearer.
They had come into the hall at the foot of
the stairs. Sonny's given me away, she
thought bitterly; he's told the cop I'm here.
That's what she got for thinking she could
trust somebody. Trying not to panic, she silently went up the iron staircase to the cupola, still carrying her shoes. She tried the
door. It creaked as it swung open. Hastily
she stopped it with her hand, then moved it
very slowly until it was just wide enough to
let her in. She closed the door behind her.

Before she could even look around, there
was a great swoosh as something flew past
her head. Stifling a scream, she sank down on
the floor, covering her head with her arms.
The sound was repeated. She made herself
look. Some hideous creature was flying back
and forth, hitting against the ceiling. Then it
settled down on the top of a window frame.
It looked like a mouse with wings. Gail
thought she was going to throw up. She
couldn't have been more scared if she had

come across a live dragon, breathing fire. But she held herself still, clenching her teeth so hard they hurt. It came to her; it was a bat. She'd never seen one, but she'd heard about them, of course. Everybody had heard about bats.

She relaxed a little, still keeping a watchful eye on the creature. It was only an animal, she told herself; it couldn't be as dangerous as a cop that was out to get you. Weren't bats blind? That was why it had banged into the ceiling. Poor dumb old bat! She looked around. The room had not been dusted in a long time. There were dead flies on the floor near the windows. A row of red clay pots stood along the wall, nothing in them but dirt. Two faded calendars were thumbtacked to the wall, one with a picture of an old-fashioned train winding along a narrow gorge, the other with a picture of a girl in weird clothes and a very big hat. The dates on the calendars were 1923 and 1929. Without knowing why she did it, she looked to see what day Christmas came on, in those years. Somehow it reassured her a little to know that it had come at all.

She made her way gingerly to the bank of windows and looked out. Far below her, looking foreshortened, like those dolls she used to have that had big heads and tiny legs, she saw Mr. Sonny and the man in the green uniform. They were talking and, as she watched, Mr. Sonny turned and pointed toward the house. She ducked back, afraid they would see her. When she looked again, they were shaking hands. Clinching the deal, she thought bitterly. He's told the cop all about me. The two men stood motionless for a second in their handshake, like a TV picture where the frame suddenly freezes. Then the man got into his car and drove off. Mr. Sonny came back into the house.

Gail sat down on the dusty floor to think. The cop's going away confused her. He hadn't looked for her. Maybe he'd gone to tell Uncle Chad where she was and ask him what to do next. Then he'd be back. Uncle Chad probably couldn't come yet; that was some comfort. She could hide from the cop just by using her wits, but if Uncle Chad himself were chasing her, she knew she'd panic. Just thinking about him made her hands feel cold.

She stayed where she was for a long time, finally half dozing in the warm sunlight. The bat stirred, now and then, but he didn't leave his perch again. A moth fluttered past Gail's face, fell to the floor, rose once more, and then fell again, dead. A bee buzzed angrily against the windowpanes. The air was stifling, but she didn't dare open a window. They were casement windows that swung out, and they would be sure to be noticed if anyone were examining the house.

She got awfully hungry, but still she stayed. She found a magazine, called *Stories of the Wild West*, published in 1929. To keep herself awake, she read the whole thing, advertisements and all. Most of the stories were about improbable adventures of cowboy heroes, who always gunned down the villain. They were like bad TV Westerns. But it was better than sitting there, thinking about how lonesome and scared she was. She studied the ads for guns. She wished she had one of those Colt .45's; she could shoot her way out of here and leap on her beautiful Appaloosa and gallop away to safety and freedom. But life seemed to have been pretty dangerous in the days of the Old West, just like now, only in a different way. She wondered if anytime, anywhere, had ever been peaceful and safe. Maybe Mrs. Partridge would know from those cards of hers. Although *they* certainly seemed to be full of danger and grief. She tried to imagine a bunch of Egyptians sitting around, looking at those same symbols, back in the twelfth century or whatever. But she didn't know anything about Egyptians, except Nasser, whose picture her mother had pinned to the wall for a while because he was so handsome.

Poor Mom. All she wanted was still to be seventeen years old and pretty, with boys hanging around all the time, fighting over her. She hadn't wanted to grow up and have a kid to worry about and be a secretary and get dumped by her husband. It was enough to make you cry your heart out. But she didn't blame her father, either. An artist shouldn't have to work from nine to five in an ad agency to support a family, when all he wanted to do was paint.

Finally, when the car had not returned, she got up and went out of the tower room, noiselessly. She opened the door that led into the wing and moved along the dark, uncarpeted hall. There were more bedrooms and another bathroom with another one of those crazy tubs. The bathroom looked as if it were in use; a big towel hung over the side of the tub, and there was a toothbrush and some shaving things on the marble shelf over the sink. Christopher?

The rooms were much like the others, only not quite as large. Each had a bed, not made up, and a bureau and chairs. She didn't know much about antiques, but they looked awfully old to her.

She came to the last room. The door was slightly ajar. She gave it a little push and it swung open. It was clearly Christopher's room. Blue jeans were thrown over a chair; a pair of muddy boots lay beside the bed; the bed was made but not very neatly. The outside wall curved, and she realized she was in one of the towers that she had seen from outside the house.

Feeling guilty, Gail stepped inside. On the wall beside her there was a bookcase. She glanced at the titles. Textbooks on botany and biology; a set of field guides to birds, mammals, fish, and trees; Thoreau's *Walden*; about a dozen books on different kinds of wildlife; a collection of essays by Santayana; several books by Loren Eisley and one by Aldo Leopold; a set of Dickens.

There was an enlarged framed snapshot on the bureau. She bent forward to look at it. A man and a woman in flying clothes leaned against the wing of a small plane. The picture was blurred, but Gail could see that the man looked like an older version of Christopher. Clipped to the frame was a newspaper article, telling of the disappearance of Daniel and Covina Parks in their plane — Parks. Then it must be Christopher's mother who was a Partridge. But old Mrs. Partridge had said, "Covina died in her bed." It was a very confusing family. There was a desk under the windows, with an old typewriter, a microscope, and some drawings of plants, signed with the initials CP.

Gail jumped. She thought she heard the front stairs creak. She left the room quickly and walked toward the main hall, then stopped. She heard footsteps. She had left the door to the wing partly open. Would it be better to hide in one of the rooms or just stay still?

Someone seemed to be pushing at the door that had stuck. She could hear it grate and creak. There was a long pause. Should she make a run for it?

Too late! She heard the door squeaking shut. Then a hand appeared on the edge of the door where she stood. Slowly it was pushed open.

13

GAIL STOOD READY to make a run for it. If she took whoever it was by surprise, she could dash past him and get out of the house. She'd head into the woods and hope for the best. Sylvester was down in the yard, or had been when she last saw him. She prayed he'd be where she could grab him quickly.

Then, almost before her plan raced through her mind, the door began to close. Holding herself absolutely still, she watched it close, heard the latch click. She wondered if she had been locked in. That would be one way to be sure of her till they were ready for her. She made herself wait, recognizing finally the slow footsteps with their uneven drag on one side. The boards creaked.

Finally when there had been no sound for several minutes, she went to the door and tried the latch. To her surprise it swung open. There was no one in the hall. She went downstairs, keeping to the wall side, and glanced all around, up and down. No one was there.

On the second floor she looked up and down the hall. As she came down the stairs to the first floor, she could hear voices: Mrs. Partridge and Mr. Sonny, in the kitchen talking. The coast was clear, then, for the moment.

It wasn't hard to imagine what had happened. Mr. Sonny had told the cop she was here. The cop had taken off to tell Uncle Chad. So he'd be back, all right, maybe with a warrant for her arrest. Did they arrest kids for running away, or just haul them back?

Hearing a door open, she ducked into Mr. Sonny's pantry. She was right next to the kitchen now, and she'd have to be very careful not to make a sound. She could hear Mrs. Partridge singing in a high, sweet voice. She was singing "Loch Lomond." Feeling happy, probably because they were going to get some kind of reward from Uncle Chad for turning her in.

She looked at the things on Mr. Sonny's desk. He was very neat. There was a pile of typing paper on the right side of his typewriter, and on the left, there was the neatly stacked manuscript. She glanced at the top page. "Chapter Seven," it was headed:

The Partridge Bank, which Robert Partridge established in 1897, is still in the hands of the Partridge family. The Partridge Mercantile, however, established in 1900 by the same Robert Partridge, was sold to out-of-state interests when Sunderlin Partridge, who was managing it, suffered an incapacitating stroke, shortly after an automobile accident in which his wife, Estelle Goulding Partridge, and his only child, Sunderlin Partridge, Jr., aged fifteen, were killed.

The rest of the page was blank. Sunderlin? Sonny? She looked at a cork bulletin board over the desk. In the center was a snapshot of a woman in a pair of saddle pants and a heavy sweater, and a boy about twelve years old. They were laughing. Three typed sentences were tacked to the cork board. One of them said, "Anyone who imagines that all fruits ripen at the same time as the strawberries knows nothing about grapes. — Paracelsus." The second one said, "You know the heart of the stranger, for you were strangers in the land of Egypt; therefore love the stranger. — Old Testament." And the third: "We go into the same river, and yet not in the same, it is we and it is not we. — Heraclitus."

Gail shook her head. This whole family was simply unreal. She was tiptoeing back into the hall, when, suddenly, the door from the kitchen opened. She froze. It was Mr. Sonny. He looked surprised, but all he said was, "Ah, there you are. I was afraid you might have wandered off into the woods and gotten lost."

"No," she said, "I was just . . . uh . . . looking around the house. Admiring the house. I guess I opened the wrong door."

"I was wondering if I should go rescue your cat," he said, in his slow, labored way. "I think the rooster is pestering him."

"Oh, I'll get him." It was a good excuse to get out of the house before the cop came back. She followed him into the kitchen. Mrs. Partridge was sitting up in bed, a white fluffy shawl around her shoulders, her hair in two tiny pigtails with blue ribbons.

"There you are," she said, in her chirpy voice. "Sonny is making his special blueberry buckle for you."

"Oh," Gail said. She could smell whatever it was — blueberry buckle? It smelled wonderful. She looked at Mr. Sonny. The stiff side of his face was toward her, expressionless, the eyelid drooping a little.

"I'd better take care of my cat." She hurried out into the yard. Sylvester lay sprawled full length on the limb of a tree, keeping his eyes on the big white rooster that strutted up and down beneath him.

"Scat!" Gail said to the rooster. She flapped her arms at him. He lifted his wings and stared at her haughtily. "Beat it! Scat!"

The rooster retreated with dignity, as if it had been his own idea. Gail reached up and hauled down the reluctant Sylvester and ran down the path Christopher had taken that other morning.

She snatched a couple of green apples from one of the bent old trees and stuffed them in her pocket. At the edge of the garden, where the path plunged at once into the forest, she found that the two basenjis were following her, eager for a romp. She ordered them back, but they just looked at her quizzically. They struck her as being more like headstrong children than dogs. "Back!" she said again. "Go home." Finally she picked up a stick and threw it back into the garden. As they dashed after it, she ran. She didn't have much hope that they wouldn't come racing after her with the stick, but then she heard someone back at the house whistle. Mr. Sonny was calling the dogs. She wondered if basenjis could track people, the way bloodhounds did. She was certain they were smart enough; it would be a question of whether they wanted to do it.

A cool wind had come up quickly; it sighed and moaned so heavily through the trees that she couldn't hear much else. She strained her ears, trying to tell whether Mr. Sonny or anyone was after her. Mr. Sonny could never catch her, not with that game leg of his, but he could send the cop.

She took a narrow trail that branched off the main path. It was overhung with evergreens that scratched her as she hurried along. Sylvester mewed and struggled, wanting to get down; but, if she let him down, he'd probably take off after a field mouse or something. She held him tighter in spite of his protests.

"Listen," she murmured in his ear, "if we stay out of sight during the day and sneak back into the house at night, the way we did at first, maybe we can make it. But we can't just stay there like sitting ducks." She bit hungrily into the hard green apple. Its sourness puckered her mouth but she ate it anyway, saving the other one for supper. Her nose twitched with the memory of the smell of blueberry buckle.

She came to a river. That was good; she could follow the river and then she wouldn't get lost. She put Sylvester down, with a command to stay close to her. He drank daintily from the stream, then shook each front paw in turn. A frog croaked. Sylvester crouched, as if ready to spring, but Gail knew he wasn't about to jump into any water. She sat down on a hummock. It was dim in the woods, the sun filtering through wherever there was a small opening in the trees. The water, running on a yellow gravel bottom, looked golden. Some very pretty white flowers grew out of the steep bank on the other side.

She was trying to think what to do about getting a message to her father. If she could find a phone booth, she could send a telegram, but where did you find a phone booth in this godforsaken wilderness? There was no phone at the Partridges. They probably hadn't heard that it had been invented.

A sudden crashing in the brush behind her brought her leaping to her feet. She grabbed Sylvester and ran along the river path, without a backward glance. The path was uneven and rough. Several times she tripped and nearly fell, but fear kept her going.

She raced around a bend and slammed into Christopher. He had been bending over, putting a trout into his creel. The impact knocked him over backward, and Gail too fell, into a prickly juniper bush. She was too startled to speak.

"Get that cat!" Christopher scrambled to his feet. "Don't let him get my fish."

Gail lunged for Sylvester, as Christopher retrieved the fish that had been knocked out of his hands. Carefully, he laid it in the creel on top of several others. Then he sat back on his heels and looked at Gail.

"I thought you were leaving."

"Well, I'm not there. I'm here."

"I told you to clear out."

"They wanted me to stay."

He made an impatient gesture. "Of course they did. They get lonesome. And they're naturally hospitable."

"Why are you so anxious to get rid of me?"

"Because I think you're in some kind of a mess, and I don't want them mixed up in it."

She laughed scornfully. "Don't worry. Your uncle can take care of himself."

"What do you mean by that?"

"He's already got the cops after me. He knows he'll get a reward. That's how people are — they're all treacherous, and you'll be just the same."

He stared at her, and then laughed. "So he's got the cops after you, has he? How'd he get in touch with them? There's no phone, you know. Do you think he walked the seven miles to the police station, with that paralyzed leg? And the reward — yeah! He's only got so much money, he couldn't spend it all if he lived to be a thousand."

"Then what's he doing, living in the kitchen?"

"It's *comfortable*." He glared at her.

"Why doesn't he put in electricity and get a bunch of servants, if he's so rich?"

"Where do you think this is, Hollywood?"

They both looked up at a sound in the brush.

"There!" Gail whispered. "They're after me. I told you."

Silently, Christopher parted the bushes and peered through them. Then he turned to her with a grin, took her arm and pulled her over to where she could see. A doe and a fawn were browsing, nibbling at the bark on a birch tree. The doe's head came up quickly as she caught their scent. With the fawn close at her heels, she leaped away from them, crashing through the brush. "There's your cop," Christopher said.

Gail's relief was almost outweighed by her amazement at seeing real deer. "They were deer!"

"What'd you expect — elephants?"

"I never saw any deer before, except in the zoo."

"There seems to be a lot you haven't seen, or heard of, or thought of." He began to take his fishing rod apart. "What's the matter with you, anyway? What are you so scared of?"

She longed to tell him. Just to get it all off her mind, into words. But she didn't really trust him. "It could have been you that told the cop."

"Sure. I sent a fish with the message. Look, kid, there is no cop."

"Oh, yes, there is. I saw him. He drove right up to your house, and Mr. Sonny was talking to him."

He looked puzzled. "What'd he look like?"

"He was in a regular cop car with the state seal on it, and he wore a green uniform, and. . . ."

"A green uniform?"

"That's what I said."

He laughed. "That was Sargent from Fish and Game. He probably came by to see if I wanted to go fishing."

She looked at him, not sure whether or not he was telling the truth. "He looked like a cop."

"I'll have to tell him. He'll be flattered. The cops around here wear khaki uniforms."

"Oh."

He finished putting his gear together and stood up.

"Where are you going?" she asked suspiciously.

"Home. I'm hungry."

She felt her stomach cave in at the word. "So am I."

He stopped and looked at her. "Tell me one thing: is that your father in the hospital?"

"No!"

Her voice held so much horror that he held up his hand. "All right, I just asked. Whoever he is, is he — or both of you — mixed up in anything crooked?"

She had to laugh. His suspicions were almost as bad as her own. "Of course not. He's just ... he is just a mean man, that's all." She felt she owed him at least that much explanation.

"All right. Then come on home." He led the way down the path, holding back the bigger branches so they wouldn't hit her in the face.

Just as they were coming near the Partridges' garden, Christopher stopped suddenly. Gail bumped into him, but he held out his arm warningly. Up at the house someone was talking to Mr. Sonny, someone with a loud, hoarse voice.

Christopher looked around quickly, then pulled her over to a tree. "Climb up," he whispered.

"I never climbed a tree," she said. She looked at it helplessly.

"Well, you're going to now." He seized her around the knees and boosted her up into the lower branches. She got a foothold on a branch and pulled herself up higher. He picked up Sylvester and handed him up to her. "Stay still." He disappeared.

It was a strange sensation, sitting in a tree, with the wind blowing and nothing visible, except more branches. Sylvester squirmed but she held him tight, and put her hand around his mouth in case he should decide to mew. She heard the hoarse voice, much nearer now. "Hi, Chris!"

When Christopher answered, it was in a voice louder than his natural one. Gail knew he meant her to hear. "Well, Sheriff Aronson. To what do we owe the pleasure?"

"Well, I was looking for this kid. . . ."

"What kid?"

"Kid that was in the car that had a wreck, the night it snowed."

"Oh, was there a kid?"

The man sounded impatient. "Chris, don't you never read the papers?"

"Not often."

"Man, you Partridges are unreal." The sheriff had moved a little, and Gail could see the top of his bald head as he took off his hat. "I was just trying to ask your Uncle Sonny if he'd seen a kid. After all, the accident was right up there on the road. This is a natural place for her to go."

"Had he seen her?" Christopher sounded polite but bored.

"Lord, how do I know? I couldn't get through to him. Say, his hearing has really gone, hasn't it?"

"He doesn't hear as well as he used to."

"You can say that again." He mopped the top of his head with his handkerchief. "I remember when I was just a little shaver and he was the big shot, running the Mercantile. He gave me a job, emptying the trash cans down to the store." He laughed. "He ain't givin' out jobs these days."

Christopher's voice was suddenly sharp. "He's had a few things happen to him since then."

"And old Mrs. Partridge, in there sound asleep in the kitchen. Can't get a rise out of *her*."

"She's ninety years old. Do you expect her to sit up and do tricks?"

"Hey, you're gettin' to be a pretty funny

fella, Chris." The sheriff laughed but he didn't sound amused. "Well, I take it you ain't seen any kid around here."

"No kid in his right mind would hang around with us," Chris said. Gail noticed the masculine pronoun and silently applauded. He was putting that dumb sheriff off the track.

"It's a she," the sheriff said. "And why wouldn't she?"

"Everybody knows this is a haunted house. You know that, Sheriff. Kids can hardly wait for Halloween to come and scare themselves to death."

The sheriff chuckled. "Guess you're right, at that. My own kids been out here a time or two."

Gail heard a scratching sound at the bottom of the tree. She carefully moved a branch with one hand and looked down. Her heart jumped. The two basenjis were standing on their hind legs, pawing at the truck. They had discovered her. Sylvester strained to break loose. Gail clung to him, holding him with one hand and her chin, while she held onto the tree with her other hand.

"What's them dogs after?" The sheriff moved closer.

"Oh, a chipmunk. They've been bugging him for half an hour. Get down, Isis! Osiris, down! Go into the house." Christopher came over and clapped his hands at them. "Beat it!"

They didn't want to go, and Gail remembered that they could climb trees. But Christopher kept at them till they bounded away toward the house.

"You Partridges can't even keep regular dogs," the sheriff said. "What breed are them dogs, anyway?"

"Basenjis."

"Why don't you get a dog you can hunt with?"

"I don't like to hunt. But if I did, a basenji can out-hunt your Irish setters any day in the week."

The sheriff exploded with laughter. "That's what you say! Them little freaks?"

"Them little freaks are the favorite hunting dog of Africa."

"Oh, Africa. What do they know?"

Christopher was leading the sheriff away from the tree, getting him off into a discussion of hunting dogs. Gail began to breathe more easily. But, just at that moment, Sylvester took advantage of her relaxed hold. He leaped for the ground and landed just behind the sheriff.

The sheriff whirled around, his hand on

his gun. "Whew! A cat. I thought it was some darned cougar or something. What a big cat!"

"Someday, I'll take the basenjis out and we'll have a contest with your setters," Christopher said.

"Wait a minute. Wait just a little old minute. That kid, the one I'm looking for, she had a big old cat."

"Arnie, you're beginning to sound like some private eye on TV."

"Where'd you get that there cat?"

"How do I know? He wandered in. Cats wander in here all the time. Uncle Sonny feeds them, they stay a while, and then they hit the road, to tell other cats that the Partridges are an easy touch." In a different tone, he said, "Scat, Jeremiah! Get out of here before the rooster eats you up."

"Jeremiah? Cat's name is Jeremiah?"

"So he says."

There was a pause. Gail couldn't see them now, so she didn't know what was happening.

"Got it here in the notes that the kid's cat is named Sylvester."

"Well, there you are, Arnie. You're barking up the wrong cat."

Their voices grew fainter, but Gail heard the sheriff say, "Just don't pull any big jokes on me, Chris. I don't take to that."

"I know, Arnie. You were never famed for your sense of humor."

Gail parted the branches and peered out. The big man had opened the door of the police car. "Why don't you get a job, Chris? You Partridges above workin', nowadays?"

Christopher's voice was cold. "I have a job."

"Oh, sure. Some government handout to draw pretty pictures of bluebells. That's what's wrong with this country, givin' federal money to guys like you that don't need it."

"I'm not on a federal grant, if you really want to know. It's simply an assignment."

"Drawin' bluebells?"

"Yeah, drawin' bluebells." Christopher turned on his heel and went into the house.

The sheriff looked after him for a moment, then got into his car and drove off, scattering a shower of gravel from under the wheels.

14

BEFORE GAIL COULD GET DOWN from the tree, Christopher came out again. "Stay up there a few minutes," he said. "Arnie likes to play tricks."

Gail groaned. It was uncomfortable in the tree and her hands were sticky with resin. "How long?"

"I'll give you the word." He left quickly.

Gail moved to another, sturdier branch, and tried to make herself more comfortable. She would do what Christopher advised; he had just gotten rid of the cop for her.

From her new seat she had a clearer view. She could see Christopher sitting on the back steps, cleaning his fish with a long, curved knife that looked like a stiletto or something. A dandy weapon, if anybody needed a weapon. Although she didn't think she could ever bring herself to cut into anything, either fish or cop. Even cutting up a steak made her uneasy. Her mother had told her once there was some kooky reason for it that came from her early childhood, but she never could remember what it was.

She was beginning to get restless, and she was about to call to Christopher to see if it was okay to come down, when she heard a car. She pulled her head back and waited. It was the sheriff again. Christopher had been right.

The sheriff got out, leaving his engine running. He looked sharply all around.

Christopher looked up at him. "Forget something, Arnie?"

"Left my hat someplace." The sheriff ran his hand over his head. "I kinda remembered I took it off when I was talkin' to you."

"Is that right?" Christopher got up and stretched, the fish knife still in his hand. He sauntered over to the sheriff's car and looked in the back seat. "This it?" He held up the hat.

For a second the sheriff didn't respond. Then he slapped his leg and roared with laughter. "By gum, that's a good one! Right in the back. And I never thought to look."

Christopher tossed it to him. The sheriff had to reach quickly to catch it. "I hope you're better at finding wicked criminals than at finding hats." He went back to his fish cleaning, ignoring the sheriff.

Gail couldn't see the sheriff's face, but she could see anger in the set of his back. He stalked back to his car. Sylvester bolted down out of his favorite willow tree and loped after him. The sheriff turned sharply and stared at the car. "What'd you say that cat's name is?"

"Jedediah."

"Yeah?"

Gail caught her breath. There was triumph in the sheriff's voice.

"Thought you said it was Jeremiah."

After a tiny second, Christopher said calmly, "Oh, one of those prophets. I didn't know you were a cat fancier, Arnie."

"I'm mighty interested in a cat named Sylvester." He leaned down stiffly. "Here, kitty, here, Sylvester."

Christopher laughed. "Any cat'll come if you call 'kitty.' "

"Here, Sylvester. Come here, boy."

But Sylvester only sat back on his hind legs and stared coldly at the sheriff. Gail could hardly keep from laughing. Sylvester wasn't just anybody's cat.

After a minute, the sheriff straightened up with a faint groan, adjusted the belt that spanned his considerable waist, and got into his car. He gunned the engine and took off.

In a little while, Sylvester went over to Christopher.

"Good cat," Christopher said. "Smart old boy." He gave him some of the leavings from the cleaned fish. Then he came over to the tree. "Come on down."

Gail followed him into the kitchen. The wind had gone down to a faint breeze, and the backyard was luminous with late afternoon light. Inside the kitchen the sunshine lit on the geraniums, picking up their color. The blueberry buckle was cooling on the shelf. Mrs. Partridge sat at the table, her hands folded, looking dreamily at the geraniums. Mr. Sonny had a pan heating for the fish, and there was a wonderful smell of fresh greens cooking. Gail couldn't tell whether it was spinach or Swiss chard or what, but she could hardly wait to eat it. She loved greens so much that her father used to call her Popeye when she was a little girl. She wondered how long before he'd come.

"Those are splendid trout, Christopher," Mrs. Partridge said.

"Rainbows," he said.

Gail looked at them and felt sorry that they weren't still darting along the golden stream. But they would taste awfully good. People are awful, she thought, me included.

"The sheriff came back?" Mr. Sonny made it sound halfway between a question and a statement.

Christopher grinned. "He forgot his hat. I found it for him. In the back seat of his car."

"Oh, good!" Mr. Sonny's face showed no knowledge of the reason for the sheriff's appearances.

"One must take into account," Mrs. Partridge said, "that he had no proper bringing-up."

"Oh, Gran," Christopher said. "You forgive everybody for everything."

"But it's true. His father drank heavily, and his poor mother did the books at the Mercantile."

Christopher laughed again. "Is doing the books at the Merc the signal for a blighted childhood?"

"No, dear, but you see she was never home. All those children and no care." She tilted her small head back, smiling a little at some far-off memory. "She was not terribly quick at the books, but Sonny thought she needed the job. All those children to feed."

"Well, Arnold has a secure job now," Sonny said. "I'm sure he does his job."

"He's evil, isn't he?" Gail said.

"No," Christopher said, "just stupid." He got up and pulled out silverware and the plates and set them out on the table. "What did Sarge want?"

"He thought you might like to go fishing Sunday. And he was asking about your experiment with the little bat."

Christopher nodded.

"There's a bat up in that big cupola." Gail was sorry at once that she'd given herself away. "I was just looking around," she added. "You said to. . . ."

"Of course, child," Mrs. Partridge said. "It's an interesting old house. Look all you want."

"I thought I got all the bats out of there," Christopher said.

"It bangs around a lot," Gail said. "They're blind, aren't they?"

"Yes, but they have very sensitive radar. It shouldn't be banging into things. Don't go in there for a while. It might be rabid."

Gail wasn't sure he had given her the real reason. "Can I see the baby bat?"

He shrugged. "Sometime."

She wondered where he kept it; but he seemed suddenly aloof, and she was afraid to ask any more questions.

After dinner, when he had washed the dishes and she had dried them, Christopher disappeared. Gail didn't know what to do. Mrs. Partridge fell asleep. Mr. Sonny stood with his back to the stove, smiling at her with the good side of his face, as if he didn't quite know what to do with her.

"Would it be all right if I borrowed a book from your library?" Gail asked.

"Certainly. Certainly." He seemed relieved. "I'll light a lamp and a fire for you."

When he had the fire going, he said, "If the light isn't strong enough, you just turn it up a little, here." He showed her. It began to smoke a little, and he turned it down again. "Too much smoke if it gets too high."

"Haven't you ever had electricity?" Gail asked.

"No. I wanted to have the house wired when I came back here to live, after my . . . after I was ill. But Mother likes to keep it the way it's always been. She lives in the past a good deal."

"Yes, I can tell." She was almost sorry she had suspected him of evil things. He had protected her when the sheriff came, and he was really being nice to her.

When he had gone, she looked around the room for something to read. She was tired of

131

Bleak House. She took down a book on Egypt and looked up Isis and Osiris. Isis, it said, was the nature goddess, whose cult started sometime between 1700 and 1100 B.C. She was the wife and sister of Osiris. Wife and sister? Gail raised her eyebrows. Things must have been different in those days. Isis was the mother of all and the mistress of all magic. Aha!

She turned to Osiris. Son of the earth god and the sky god, father of Horus, the sun of a new day. Osiris was the creative force that gave life to seeds and immortality to all things. He was killed by his brother Set, god of evil.

She read a little more and then put the book back. Well, it was nice to know that, although the Partridge family included dogs named Isis and Osiris, as far as she knew there was nobody named Set.

She found a slim book on the history of the region she was in. It was stiffly and uninterestingly written, but there were frequent allusions to the early members of the Partridge family, and pictures of the house when it was first built, a later picture of the formal gardens, showing a little summerhouse near where the Cupid now stood, and some pictures of the Partridge Bank and the Partridge Mercantile. She leafed through the book sleepily, looking for pictures and thinking dreamily of how good Mr. Sonny's blueberry buckle had been. She slid down onto the comfortable rug in front of the fire and leaned her head back against the ottoman.

When she was almost asleep, the book fallen to the floor beside her, she thought she heard music. She opened her eyes and sat up to listen. Yes, someone was playing the piano. Probably a radio, she thought; Christopher probably had a transistor. But it didn't sound like a radio. It sounded real. Then the music stumbled, paused, and began again, and she knew that someone was in the ballroom playing the piano.

She opened the library door. It was beautiful music but somehow imperfect, with occasional breaks and pauses. She sat down on the lower step of the wide stairway to listen. It must be Christopher, but she knew instinctively that he wouldn't want her to come up there. Anyway, it was nice to listen in the old hallway, with the light from her library lamp making a pale pattern on the floor. Gail liked music. Her mother always said that if her father would send the money, she could take piano lessons. Gail didn't know whether he'd sent it or not, but she'd never gotten the lessons. The FM band on the radio at home was the best she could find in the way of music.

This was a kind of music she'd never heard before, plaintive and haunting, almost as if some lonesome ghost had wandered into the ballroom and was remembering old times. It didn't sound like Christopher. She stirred a little uneasily and wished she'd brought Sylvester with her to the library. But he had been sleeping so comfortably under the kitchen stove, she hadn't wanted to disturb him.

A stair creaked just behind her. She turned her head so quickly that it gave her a crick in her neck.

"I didn't mean to scare you." It was Christopher. He sat down on the step above her. "I came down to listen."

She was bewildered and a little angry, now that she saw she had been foolish to be frightened. "I thought you were playing the piano."

He shook his head. "I can't play like that."

"Then who is it?"

"Uncle Sonny." He winced as the music broke off on a wrong note and began again. "It's very hard for him. After his stroke, he had to learn all over again. He plays almost

134

everything with just his right hand, and a few easy chords in the bass with his left. . . ." He listened intently. "The man's so good. He could have been a concert pianist."

Gail relaxed. With the mystery and its tinge of fear cleared up, she could just concentrate on the music. For a few moments, it was lively and gay, then it went into a passage so limpid and pure that it made Gail see the forest again: tall green trees, green ferns, a golden stream rushing along between high banks. . . .

When it stopped, she let out a long breath and let her head fall back, as if she had no strength left.

In a low voice, Christopher said, "That's one kind of magic, isn't it?"

Into the silence, from somewhere outside the house, came a long, unearthly wail. Shocked out of her reverie, Gail jumped up. A second wail followed. It was like the scream of a banshee, not of this world. "What is it!"

Christopher, on his feet, caught her arm. He pressed a flat key into her hand. "It's the dogs. Somebody's out there. Go up to my lab and lock yourself in."

"Lab?" she said blankly.

"The room on the third floor. Hurry up!"

He jumped the lower steps and disappeared in the direction of the kitchen. As she raced up the stairs, Gail saw the ballroom doors begin to open. But she didn't wait. She went on up to the third floor. The lab must be the room with the stuck door. She went up to it and pushed hard. The door gave way and she went inside. It was pitch dark and there were strange noises.

15

GAIL LOCKED THE DOOR from the inside and
huddled against it in the dark. The room was
dense with darkness, not even a glimmer of
light to show the windows. She realized they
must be curtained. There was a strange smell
that she couldn't identify, and there were
peculiar sounds, one of them a soft repeated
click and, in between the clicks, a noise like
escaping steam. The smell of the room, she
decided, was like the woods, like a patch of
wet grass or weeds. She wished Christopher
would come. Who could have driven in?

She sat very still, trying not to get nervous.
At least no one could break in on her. She
had left the key in the lock. But the room
itself made her jumpy. She wished she could
turn on a light. Although even if there were
one, it would be a reckless thing to do. Anyone outside would spot it at once.

She tried to think of pleasant things, but she couldn't find too many to think of, right offhand. She wished she knew how her mother was. That worry stayed constantly in the back of her mind. Mom would be awfully mad when she heard Gail had run away from Uncle Chad. She hoped he hadn't sent her word.

As her eyes became accustomed to the darkness, she could make out the edges of the windows and the dark shape of the curtains. This was another one of the rooms that had a curved outside wall.

She jumped at the sound of a small thump near her; and a moment later a short, rasping cluck-cluck-cluck sounded very near her. She shuddered and moved away. In her imagination, the room began to fill with all sorts of strange and frightening creatures. Gail held her breath, afraid something would touch her. If only Sylvester were there. . . . She had the awful feeling that if anything alive touched her, she would scream. She wondered if her mother felt like this, when her nerves began to go. She felt a new rush of sympathy for her. Things could keep on happening to you until you just couldn't stand it any longer.

But she couldn't act like this. She hugged her knees up tight to her chest and spoke aloud, quietly. "All right, whatever is in this room, just keep your distance. I'm not going to bother you, you don't bother me, all right?" She felt a little better. The sound of her own voice was somehow reassuring. After all, Christopher wouldn't send her to a room that had dangerous things in it. But she knew it wasn't really dangerous things that she was worried about; it was creepy things. And Christopher's idea of creepy, she suspected, would not be the same as hers.

She clenched her teeth and began to count in French. It was almost the only thing she could do in French, and she had been using it as a pacifier ever since the sixth grade. When she reached *cinquante et un*, there was a quiet knock on the door. She sat still, not answering. It could be anybody.

Then Christopher's voice said, "It's me. Unlock the door."

She was surprised to see how badly her hands shook. She had thought the French numbers had quieted her down. Christopher came in, carrying a lighted Coleman lantern, which he put down on the floor just inside the door.

"Who was it?"

"Arnie."

"Again?"

"Yeah. He said your uncle wanted him to

check back and give us a description of you, so if you showed up we could let him know." He grinned. "He says you're small and skinny and you've got freckles."

Gail felt depressed. If this was to be the pattern, popping up every few hours, sooner or later he'd catch up with her. "I guess I'd better go away," she said. "He'll catch me one of these times."

"He will probably hang around in the vicinity, but he won't come to the house again."

"How do you know?"

"Uncle Sonny told him off. He was magnificent. Uncle Sonny has a law degree from Stanford, among other things, and he quoted chapter and verse on invasion of privacy, harassment, et cetera, et cetera. I don't know if he was making it up or not, but he impressed Arnie."

She leaned against the wall. "I don't know what to do." She was afraid she was going to cry.

"That guy in the hospital. Who is he?"

"My uncle." Speaking quickly, to get it over with, she said, "He is a wicked, mean man. My mother is in a mental hospital, and my father is in Hawaii. He hasn't lived with us for years. So my uncle got a court order to take me home with him. When the car crashed, I ran away. I would have run away, somehow, or else killed myself."

"Are you sure you aren't exaggerating?"

"No," she said.

He didn't speak for a moment. When he did, his voice was casual. "Well, you'd better stay here for now. Till your father comes, or whatever." He picked up the lantern. "Would you like to see the baby bat?"

"I think so. Things have been making funny noises. I was scared."

He laughed. "Here's the bat."

It was a tiny brown shapeless thing, curled into a mound of cotton on the bottom of a glass jar. She stared at it. "Are you going to keep it forever?"

"Oh, no. I'll let him go when he's big enough to take care of himself. He'll live in the woods or find himself a cave. He's called the Little Brown Myotis." He turned to a big table. There were several fern leaves spread out and pencil drawings of the leaves. Tall glass jars held sprays of weeds, some with tiny brown globes on the stems, some fringed and tasseled. He pointed to a big glass jar. "Here's a young wood frog."

She had to get close to see him. He was huddled in a bunch of damp leaves and small

141

stones. He had a broad, flat, reddish body and a pointed head with protruding eyes that peered up at them. "Is he the one that goes cluck-cluck-cluck?"

"He's the one."

"And something else sounds like a tea kettle steaming."

He moved the light. "That's my tiger salamander."

She looked at the strange, yellow-blotched creature with the long tail, and shivered. "Will he bite?"

"Oh, no. Salamanders are good guys."

"Why do you keep these things up here?"

"I draw them. I'm having trouble with the frog. I'm a lot better at vegetation than I am at animals. I don't get the anatomy right. I may have to take an art course this winter."

"My father is an artist."

"Is he? Is he good?"

"I don't know. He thinks he is."

He smiled. "Well, Gran is waiting for us to come and have a cup of tea." He led the way to the door.

"Is she going to tell any more fortunes?"

"I don't think so."

Mr. Sonny was popping corn. He smiled at them over his shoulder, as he shook an old corn popper back and forth over the banked fire in the stove. Butter was melting in a little pan. The popcorn smelled wonderful. Sylvester dozed near the warm stove, his head pushed up against Isis.

Mrs. Partridge sat up straight in her chair, her feet not quite touching the floor. She looked bright eyed and pleased with life. "Your mother," she said to Christopher, "loved popcorn more than anything on this earth."

Gail saw the quick flash of pain in his eyes before he turned his head away.

"That was the other Covina, Gran," he said gently. "It was Great-aunt Covina who loved popcorn."

Mrs. Partridge looked bewildered for a moment. "My Covina. Yes." She sighed deeply. "My dear, fun-loving Covina. Died in her bed. Thirty-three years old."

So there were two Covinas. For just a second, Gail had a vivid sense of the presence of Great-aunt Covina, young and full of fun and loving popcorn, making popcorn right here in this kitchen on that same stove. The whole rush and sweep of life seemed to swirl all around her — people now, people then. . . . It was like a play, where the stage darkened for a moment and then the lights came up on other characters; yet, somehow, all of them closely linked together. She had never experienced anything like it before. Even her own grandmother, whom she had known so well, she had hardly thought of, once she was dead. Now it occurred to her that part of her was her grandmother.

"Shake the salt with a light hand, Christopher," Mr. Sonny said in a cheerful voice.

"Keep an eye on me, Gran. See if I use a light enough hand."

Mrs. Partridge brightened again, and Gail thought this must be an old family joke that they had brought up to take her mind off Covina.

"One grain of salt to every kernel of corn," she said. She laughed her gay, tinkly laugh. "One to one, Christopher, my dear." She leaned forward to watch him as he pretended to measure out the salt in that proportion.

Christopher set small bowls in front of each of them and pushed the salt cellar toward Gail. "Most people want a touch more than Gran's formula."

"Too much salt spoileth the corn." Mrs. Partridge laughed and popped some of the corn into her mouth. Daintily she wiped melted butter from her chin.

"Is that an old proverb, Gran?"

"It ought to be, if it isn't."

Mr. Sonny sat down beside them. "If the salt hath lost its savor, wherewith shall the corn be salted?"

They all laughed as if they were very happy. Gail found herself wanting to giggle, too. She loved nonsense. She wondered if they ever read Lewis Carroll. " 'Twinkle, twinkle, little bat!' " she began.

Mr. Sonny beat out the rhythm on the table. " 'How I wonder what you're at!' "

Christopher pointed upward. " 'Up above the world you fly, like a tea-tray in the sky.' "

Mrs. Partridge clapped her hands in delight. " 'Off with his head! He's murdering the time!' "

They all laughed very hard and ate popcorn very fast.

16

THE DAYS WENT BY in a pleasant flow of good weather and reassuring routine. Waked by the big white rooster every morning, she had breakfast with Mrs. Partridge and Mr. Sonny. Christopher had gone away again, with his backpack, his camera, and his sketchbook, to work on his project.

After breakfast, Gail worked for a while in the garden with Mr. Sonny, helping him water the new rows of beans that Christopher had set out and weed and water the rest of the garden. The peas had come up and were starting to blossom; beets were in the tiny stage, ready to eat, greens and all; radishes were ready to pull up. Gail got to know the different vegetables and to watch eagerly each day for new developments. Sometimes, Sylvester had to be driven away from the garden, because he liked to dig and roll in the warm dirt.

The basenjis teased him and chased him

and were in turn chased, all three of them racing up tree trunks and leaping off branches. Watching them, Gail thought Sylvester hadn't had so much fun since he was a kitten. He had run off some of his fat and his coat had become glossy. He still treated the rooster with respect, but even the rooster seemed to have grown used to the cat, only flapping his wings and darting at him if he came too close. The hens scattered and flapped and squawked whenever he came near, but they forgot him at once, busy with their constant pecking.

Gail had learned how to collect eggs without causing too much anguish in the hen-house. She scattered corn on the picnic table and watched the hens eat, knowing now who ate first, who last. She gave the hens names — Guinevere, Julie Andrews, Alice, Myrtle, Patty Jo, Miss Bullitt, Mrs. Abrams. Miss Bullitt was the mean one. Gail called the rooster simply His Majesty.

She liked working with Mr. Sonny. He didn't talk much, but he was never impatient if she did anything wrong, and he didn't treat her like a dumb kid. Also she noticed that he kept a sharp lookout for anyone who might approach the place. Every afternoon he walked up to the road to get the mail, and he always let her know right away that nothing had come yet from her father.

"Mail is slow," he would say. "And Hawaii is a long way off."

But there should have been time to get some word back if her father were still there. She began slowly to wonder if he would really come to save her. It had been an awfully long time since he had seen her; maybe he didn't even think about her anymore, although she thought about him all the time. Maybe he wouldn't want to be bothered with some kid he couldn't even remember. But she tried not to let herself think such things. Instead she remembered how kind he had always been, how much fun they had had together. The Partridges would like him, she thought. He was like them, in a way.

On Mr. Sonny's advice, she never went far from the house alone. But one morning she awoke, knowing that that day she had to go for a walk in the woods. She felt cooped up, restless. Since no one had been around in such a long time, she thought, maybe Uncle Chad had given up and gone home. In order not to worry the Partridges, she didn't mention the fact that she had decided to take a walk. She wouldn't go far, after all. She'd probably be back before they missed her.

She waited until after lunch, when Mrs.

Partridge was taking a nap and Mr. Sonny was tip-tapping away on his typewriter. Quietly she let herself out the kitchen door. She wanted to take Sylvester with her but she wasn't sure where he was. She called to him softly a few times but only the basenjis responded, racing around her in circles until she felt dizzy. "Cut it out!" she said, laughing. "Cool it, you guys."

She walked down the tangled path she had come over when she first found the Partridge place. Maybe she could help Mr. Sonny trim some of the hedges. He couldn't handle a hedge trimmer with one hand, probably, but maybe she could do it, if he told her how. It must have been pretty there in the old days. She could imagine a younger Mrs. Partridge tending the flower beds, now full of weeds. The spirea was in bloom, its delicate white blossoms scenting the air, and small flowering plum trees were hung with pink. But the ornamental evergreens had lost their form, and the privet hedge that bordered the path had grown so wild and straggly that in some places she had to stoop to get through. A good place for a cat to hide. She whistled softly and listened, but there was no answering meow.

She came to the pool, where the marble

Cupid forever bent his head over an empty basin half-full of last year's dead leaves. Gail turned over the fallen marble bench and set it right. It was heavy. She wondered how many people had sat there on a nice moonlit night and looked at the blue water of the pool and dreamed about what they were going to do with their lives. She wondered if Christopher ever came there. What would he dream about, if he did? Baby bats? Tree toads?

A path that she hadn't noticed before led off to her left into the woods, probably joining up with the one from the house. She glanced over the stone wall to the bumpy dirt road. At the same time that she saw Sylvester, lying in a patch of sunlight just this side of the stone wall, she saw the front bumper of a parked car. As she shrank back into the dense shrubbery, she heard low voices from the road.

She held her breath as two men came into view. The sheriff led the way, and just behind him was Uncle Chad, his left arm in a cast. Gail wanted more than anything to run, but she was sure they hadn't seen her yet. If she kept perfectly still, they might not see her at all. She saw Sylvester lift his head, his ears pointed forward. She wished desperately that she had found him first. The men were bound to see him.

At that moment the sheriff did see him. "There's that fool cat," he said.

Uncle Chad leaned over the wall and looked. "That's her cat."

"Knew it all the time!" The sheriff sounded triumphant. "I knew if we hung around here long enough. . . ."

"Here, kitty!" Uncle Chad held out his hand, but Sylvester stood up and stiffly walked away. Uncle Chad looked all around. "The question is, where is the girl?"

"She might be up to the house, but it'd take a squad of men to find her if the Partridges don't want to give her up."

Uncle Chad looked at him. "You're afraid of the Partridges."

The sheriff blustered. "Man, I ain't afraid of nobody. But I don't tangle with that family if I can help it."

"Well, we'll just have to keep watch. I want to find the girl. I'm responsible for her." He shot a look of contempt at the sheriff. "Since you won't issue a search warrant."

"I can't issue no search warrant on the Partridges. I'd be run out of town. Everybody likes 'em. They got influence."

"From what you tell me, I'd say they

haven't had influence for forty years."

"They still own the bank and all. Nobody's going to get away with roughing up Mr. Sonny and his mother."

At that moment Gail realized that Sylvester had discovered her. He changed his direction and started toward her hiding place.

"I'm an officer of a bank myself, since you're so impressed by banks."

"I'm only impressed by the one I owe money to," the sheriff said.

Sylvester covered the last few feet between himself and Gail with a flying leap, disturbing her cover of bushes as he did it.

Uncle Chad gave a shout. "There she is! Gail! Wait." He started to climb over the wall, clumsily because of his broken arm.

Gail stood up and tried to scoop the cat up into her arms, but he squirmed free and ran along the edge of the pool.

"Gail!" Uncle Chad called. "Stay there."

"No."

"Stay where you are, or I'll shoot your cat." The sheriff pulled his gun and aimed it at Sylvester.

To get Sylvester Gail had to run into the open, closer to the two men, who were over the wall now. But she had no choice. She ran toward Sylvester, praying he'd stand still. He did, and this time he let her pick him up. She heard a gun bark, and the plink of a bullet as it hit the marble bench. Both men were shouting at her to stop, but she ran for the woods.

She ran and ran and ran, never stopping to look back or listen. The path did connect with the one from the house. She took the same turn-off trail to the river that she had taken the day she bumped into Christopher. She thought about their being able to track her by broken bushes and that sort of thing, but there was no time to be careful. Her only hope lay in outrunning them. She was pretty sure she could outrun Uncle Chad, with his broken arm and his recent concussion, but she wasn't sure about the sheriff. He was fat and awkward, but he was local and he probably knew the woods well.

She had Sylvester slung over her shoulder. He clung tight, not trying to get loose. If he were only a magic cat! She began to make a wish: Cat, don't let them catch me . . . don't let them catch me! Don't let them, please. But Sylvester couldn't help. She was gasping for breath and sweat poured down her face, blinding her. Branches lashed against her face. But still she ran. All kinds of strange things went through her mind. She thought about how Osiris had been killed by his evil brother Set. She thought of the Five Pentacles, the shivering, ragged man and woman walking under the great lighted window and never looking up. She caught her breath in a hard sob. Would she ever get one of the good cards? Other people had good things happen to them, sometimes.

She tripped over a half-buried rock and fell. Sylvester jumped out of her arms and ran into the underbrush, then sat down and looked at her. She had trouble breathing and there was a sharp pain under her ribs. She lay still for a moment, trying to listen, trying to hear below the forest noises to the sounds of the men who were chasing her. Somewhere a twig snapped, and she cowered against the ground, shaking all over. Then she remembered the deer who had frightened her before. It wasn't necessarily Uncle Chad or the sheriff.

She sat up and held out her hand to Sylvester. He came meekly, and she picked him up again. We've got to go fast and silent like an Indian, she thought. Sylvester purred. Maybe he could read her mind. She got up and began to run again, more carefully now, trying not to crash into things. Because if she could hear them, they could hear her. Going more carefully meant going slower, but she had to make the choice. She couldn't keep up that fast pace without making a racket. Even her breathing seemed to her to fill the whole forest.

She came to a place where the stream divided, flowing around a small island of gravel and brush. She stopped. The water made a soft murmuring sound. Shadows from overhanging trees danced on its surface, and she saw a fish in the little pool that bordered the island. His tail flicked back and forth. She wondered if it were a trout. She hoped nobody would catch him.

She waded in the shallow stream for a little way, and came out on the other side. Water wouldn't show any footprints. She gasped as a big, long-tailed bird swooped through the open space above the water, flashing black and white against the blue sky.

She couldn't hear any sounds that might be people now, but she kept on going at a fast walk. The trees around here were tall, but the ground was free of brush, almost like a park. It was pretty, but it wasn't a good place to hide. She was afraid to move away from the stream, for fear of getting lost. She hurried along, glancing back over her shoulder every few minutes. It seemed to her that Uncle Chad hovered invisible, close behind her waiting for the right moment to swoop down on her. She began to think of him as a big black bird with huge talons. A dark horror almost overcame her. She could see no hope. She couldn't go on forever running through the woods like a frightened deer. And she couldn't upset the Partridge family by hiding forever in their house. Her father was probably not going to come. What would happen to her?

Sylvester squirmed, trying to get down, but she held onto him. If he got away from her, everything would be lost. He mewed, protesting.

Then Sylvester stopped squirming and turned his head, his ears forward. He had heard something. She looked around frantically for some kind of cover, but there was none. Suddenly, she heard what Sylvester was listening to. Someone was singing. Up ahead of them a clear tenor voice was singing. For a minute she thought she was losing her mind. Cautiously she moved forward, keeping close to the trees. Then she stopped. The voice seemed to be coming from the sky.

> *. . . if I live to be a hundred*
> *I will never know from where*
> *Came those ribbons, lovely ribbons,*
> *Scarlet ribbons for her hair . . .*

Gail moved silently toward the source of the music. At the foot of a tall ponderosa, she looked up. Far up, at the top of the tree, Christopher leaned against the trunk. He looked down and saw her.

"Hi," he said.

She burst into tears.

17

"COME UP," Christopher said.

She tried to stop crying. "I can't."

"Sure you can. It's an easy tree to climb. I'll give you a hand." He came partway down.

Sylvester jumped out of her arms and ran up the trunk.

"See? I told you it was easy." Christopher held out his hand.

Clumsily she climbed from one branch to the next, trying not to look down. Christopher caught hold of her arm and helped her up.

"You can't see the view if you keep on crying," he said. She swallowed hard and put her face down to wipe the tears off on her arm.

"What were you crying for?"

She clenched her teeth, afraid she was going to burst into tears again. "That song

. . . it was so beautiful. I thought you were an angel or something."

He laughed. "I am, really, when you get to know me."

"Don't joke."

"All right. What are you doing way out here? You could get lost."

"My uncle and the sheriff were chasing me. The sheriff shot at us."

"Shot at you!"

"He said he'd shoot Sylvester, so I grabbed Sylvester and ran, and he shot anyway. I heard the bullet hit your marble bench."

When Christopher spoke again, his voice had changed. "Well," he said, "I guess we've had about enough of that stuff."

She looked at him quickly. "I'll have to leave, won't I?"

"Of course not. I mean we've had enough of Arnie and his John Wayne act. When Uncle Sonny hears about this, he'll probably sue. That big fat boob can't come on our premises and shoot at people, or at cats or anything else."

"I'm getting your whole family into a mess, just the way you said I would."

"Well, there are some things a person just can't let happen." He handed her the binoculars that he'd had around his neck. "As long as you're up here, you may as well enjoy it."

As far as she could see, the forest reached, crisscrossed by streams and broken here and there by many lakes. In the distance the Rockies reared up, still capped with snow. She moved the glasses slowly, taking it all in. "It's beautiful," she said finally.

He pointed to a small lake in the near distance. "That's my project."

It was a teardrop-shaped lake, deep green, with a stream coming into it from the north and a small green swampy area to the south. Willows and birches hung over its banks.

"What do you do?"

"I'm doing an ecostudy of that area."

"What's that?"

"I study all the different kinds of life in that one area, how they relate to each other, who feeds what, how they survive or don't survive."

"You mean animals?"

"Animals, fish, plants, insects, everything."

"Is there a lot?"

"You wouldn't believe how much. Some of it too small to see without a microscope."

She gave him the glasses. "Is that fun?"

"Well, to me it's the only thing that's any real fun."

"I've never known anybody like you. I mean most boys aren't like that."

"What are most boys like, where you come from?"

"Oh, I don't know. Mean."

"Oh, well. There are mean people here, too. Look at Arnie."

She hunched up her shoulders and tried not to think about Arnie or Uncle Chad. "Why is the lake green?"

"Algae."

The light wind made the treetop sway slightly. It was both scary and nice. She hung on tight. "It's like looking down on the whole world and seeing how pretty it is."

"Yes."

"When I was a little kid, I used to want to climb onto the Flying Red Horse — you know, at the gas station? And fly to the stars. This is almost as good."

"Maybe better."

Maybe. She wasn't sure. You couldn't tell that unless you really saw the stars.

"We'd better get on home before the folks begin to worry about you."

She hung back as he held out his hand. "I'm scared to go."

"I'll be with you."

"That sheriff's got a gun."

"Look, he wouldn't have really shot you or the cat. He's stupid but not that stupid. He wanted to scare you so you'd give up."

"He'd have shot Sylvester." She leaned out to look for Sylvester. The branch cracked and she lunged for the trunk.

"Take it easy." Christopher caught her.

"Uncle Chad will take me away."

"If you don't want to go, you don't have to. You can wait for your father."

"How do you know?"

Impatiently he said, "I know. Now, come on! You can't spend the rest of your life in a tree."

"He's got a court order."

"So what? It isn't signed by God, is it? We can tell the court that your father's coming for you, if it comes to that."

She leaned her head against her arm. The pungent smell of the pine tree was so strong, she could almost taste it. "I don't think he's coming."

"Sure he is. Come on down, now."

Well, Christopher didn't know anything about it. But he was right, she couldn't stay in a tree forever. Carefully she reached her foot down for the next branch. He caught her ankle and put her foot where it ought to be. In a few minutes, she jumped the last few feet to the ground. "Come on, Sylvester," she said. She was too tired to carry him. She walked behind Christopher, trying not to think of all the awful things that could happen.

Christopher walked quickly and silently, not talking at all. Gail wished she could move that way through the woods; that would be a real advantage. She felt terribly depressed. She could see what was going to happen. No matter how long she evaded him, Uncle Chad would win in the end. She shivered.

They seemed to walk forever. It was hard to believe she had run all this way.

The woods steamed in late afternoon heat. Although the trees shut out most of the direct sunshine, the forest got hot and humid. Mosquitoes and gnats pestered her. Her left arm was swollen from mosquito bites, and bleeding from being scratched. Once, when Christopher was holding back a branch so it wouldn't fly back and hit her, he noticed her arm.

"You ought to use a repellent," he said. "They really get to you."

She noticed that they didn't seem to bother him, but she didn't have the strength to ask if he used a repellent, or what. He seemed to be so closely related to the forest, probably even the insects let him alone.

Sylvester, never a good walker, began to

stop frequently and sit down. Wearily she leaned over to pick him up.

"I'll take him." Christopher picked up the big cat and slung him over his shoulder.

Gail was amazed. Sylvester had never liked to be handled by anyone but her, but there he was, his head resting on Christopher's shoulder, staring back at her.

"Do you believe in magic?" she said.

"'There are more things in heaven and earth,' et cetera."

She knew that was from Shakespeare, or somebody like that, but she didn't know what it had to do with anything.

"Magic's just a word people used to explain what they don't understand." He came to a clearing and signaled her to stay where she was and be quiet. He circled the open space and shinnied up a tree. He was out of her sight for a few minutes.

"What is it?" she whispered when he reappeared.

He shook his head. "I just had a feeling somebody was around. You know, a creepy feeling in my skin."

She knew what he meant, and her own skin began to feel itchy and peculiar. Maybe it was just the mosquitoes.

"Better not talk anymore." He led the way,

moving more warily than ever, staying close to the big trees. She followed his lead. She wasn't as confident as he was that he could handle both the sheriff and Uncle Chad. The Partridges obviously carried weight with the sheriff, but to Uncle Chad they would just be a bunch of country kooks. She burned with indignation at this imagined insult to her friends.

Sylvester, whom Christopher had put down when he climbed the tree, lagged behind again. She picked him up, not wanting to bother Christopher with him. Sylvester was hot and heavy. She kept stumbling. All her muscles ached, and her head felt as if she had a fever. Maybe she'd get sick and have to stay in the hospital a long time, in the contagious ward where Uncle Chad couldn't get at her. Was it wicked to pray for a light case of the plague?

She was so tired, she had to keep her eyes on her feet, willing herself to put one foot forward and then the other. Her face was scratched from the branches and her hair was a tangled mess. It seemed to her that even her freckles were on fire.

Because she had her head down, she bumped into Christopher when he stopped. She recoiled violently and dropped Sylvester.

Christopher reached to catch him, but the cat disappeared in the tangle of serviceberry bushes. She was too tired to be worried.

He led her to a boulder that was braced against a big willow with low spreading branches. He parted the branches. "Sit here till I come back."

Panic rose in her throat. "Where are you going?"

"Just to get the lay of the land. I'll be right back. Nobody'll see you here, even if they were to come this way." He let the branches fall into place.

She peered at him through the soft green leaves. The idea of his leaving her alone, even for a few minutes, made her feel like fainting with terror. "Please . . ." she said hoarsely.

"It'll all be over in a few minutes," he said. His voice was kind. "Don't panic now. You've been real good." And he was gone.

Real good. More like real dead. She took off one of her sneakers and dumped out the dirt and pine needles, then thought about dumping the other one, too, but gave it up as too much work. She leaned her head back against the rough bark of the willow. "Willow, weep for me," her mother used to sing. Some old pop song. Her mother knew the

166

words of all the old pop songs, the really old
ones.

She thought about Set killing Osiris.
Tricked him into a coffer, the book said, and
nailed the lid and sealed it with molten lead.
Coffer . . . coffin? How did you trick somebody into a coffin? It didn't sound to her as if
Osiris had been too bright. Set had square
ears. That she'd like to see. She lay back, her
arms hanging wearily at her sides, trying to
imagine square ears. Ridiculous! Her eyes
closed. She forced them open. This was no
time to go to sleep. But, in spite of her efforts,
they drooped again. Her head fell to one
side, then she jerked awake. But, in a few
minutes, she was dozing again.

She woke again, taut with the sense of
danger. Near her a hand was parting the
branches. An arm appeared, encased in
white. She closed her fingers around a big
flat rock, and as a man came into the opening, she hurled it at his head. Mr. Sonny fell
forward, blood gushing from his temple.

18

GAIL BEGAN TO SCREAM for Christopher. Uncle Chad might hear her, but it didn't matter now. Mr. Sonny lay crumpled on the ground, blood from the gash on his head staining the pine needles. His eyes were closed and he didn't move. Gail knelt beside him, stroking his hair and moaning.

"I've killed him. I've killed him. He was the kindest man I ever knew, and I've killed him." She shouted again for Christopher.

In a moment she heard him coming, running through the forest, not trying now to be silent. When he broke into the clearing, he stopped short.

"Uncle Sonny!" The color drained from his face.

"I did it. I thought it was Uncle Chad. I hit him with a rock." She held Mr. Sonny's long thin hand in hers.

Very gently, Christopher knelt beside his

uncle and felt his pulse. "You didn't kill him."
He smoothed back his uncle's thin brown
hair. The bleeding was slowing down to a
trickle. "Look, don't move him. I'm going for
the doctor."

"What can I do?" Gail said. "I'll do anything...."

"Don't do a thing," he said sternly. "Not
one thing. Just stay there and be with him.
Don't touch him, don't try to move him." He
was gone before she could answer. For a few
minutes, she heard the breaking sounds of
undergrowth as he ran.

She rocked on her heels. "Please be all
right," she whispered to him. "Please be all
right. You've been so good to me. You're so
good." If Uncle Chad came now, she
wouldn't even look up. And ten Uncle Chads
couldn't take her away from Mr. Sonny. She
was no longer afraid of anything except that
Mr. Sonny might die.

He stirred a little. She held her breath,
watching him closely. He moved again and
turned his head, straightening his long legs
as he moved. He groaned softly. Then his
eyes fluttered open and he looked at her, a
bewildered look. He closed his eyes again.
But his breathing seemed deeper. Perhaps he
would be all right.

With his eyes closed and both sides of his

face still, he didn't have that look of the two parts of his face not matching. It seemed to her to be the gentlest face she had ever seen. She clenched her hands together. How could she have done such a terrible thing? Throwing a rock like that, before she had even been sure. That was what fear could do to you, fear and mistrust of everything. She was never going to allow herself to be that way again. After all, if she'd gotten away from Uncle Chad once, she could do it again. If he ended up taking her away, and if he didn't treat her right, she would just go to the police and tell them. There might be a nice policeman who would listen to her. There *were* nice men in the world. Mr. Sonny had proved that.

She took off her sweater and put it over Mr. Sonny. His eyes opened again, just a little, and he seemed to be smiling. Then he closed them and lay still. It seemed forever that Christopher had been gone. No phone. Everybody ought to have a phone. No car, either. She had seen the ten-speed bike in the barn. Probably he had taken that.

The sun's rays slanted low through the trees, and the first chill of evening came in the rising wind. She wished she had something else to keep Mr. Sonny warm. She'd heard you should keep people warm when they'd had an accident. She got up and found a broken branch of a birch tree, its leaves still green. She brought it over and carefully spread it across his chest, pulling off the leaves that might touch his face. It was probably crazy, but didn't bears use branches and things when they went to bed for the winter?

She bent over to look at the wound. It had stopped bleeding but it was a nasty gash. You could really kill somebody quick, hitting them in the temple. For a few minutes she shook so hard, her teeth chattered. She stiffened her arms and braced them against a tree until she had forced herself to stop. Why didn't Christopher come?

And then she heard voices. For a second she forgot her resolution not to be afraid. It might be the sheriff and Uncle Chad. But she stood up and called, "Over here!"

Christopher and a middle-aged man she hadn't seen before hurried into the clearing. The man carried a doctor's bag. He crouched beside Mr. Sonny, holding his pulse, touching the area around the wound with gentle fingers.

"That's a mean cut," he said.

"I did it," Gail said.

"She thought it was someone else," Christopher said.

The doctor looked up, a quick, wry grin on his face. "Someone who needed to be conked on the head?" He didn't wait for an answer. "Has he opened his eyes at all?"

"Yes, twice. He almost smiled."

"Good." He wiped the blood away from the edges of the wound and found a gauze compress in his bag. He fitted it carefully over the gash and fixed it with adhesive. "I'll want to bring him into the hospital for an x-ray, and he'll need a few days' rest and observation."

"Is he going to be all right?" Gail said.

"I think so. But we want to be sure. You help me carry him, Chris. Very carefully, now. Easy does it!"

As they lifted him, Mr. Sonny opened his eyes again. "Hello," he said, very faintly.

The doctor smiled. "Hi, Sonny. You just relax now. You got a little cut on your head. I want to fix it up."

"Yes." Mr. Sonny's voice was almost a whisper.

Gail went ahead of them, parting branches, moving stones out of their way. It seemed a long way back to the yard. She watched them lay him carefully on the back seat of the doctor's car.

"I'm going with him," Christopher said. He looked very white. "Can you tell Gran without scaring her?"

"Yes. Yes, I will."

"Don't scare her, you hear?"

"No, I won't. Honest."

Still Christopher hesitated. "Maybe I should tell her myself."

"Let's get Sonny into the hospital," the doctor said. "The girl will explain to Mrs. Partridge. Tell her Sonny got a cut on his head, but he's going to be all right. Pulse is just a little weak, but nothing serious. No sign of another stroke. Stay with her."

"Oh, I will." As soon as the car started up the drive, Gail ran to the house. She stopped a second before she opened the door, to pull herself together. She mustn't act nervous.

Mrs. Partridge was sitting at the table, watching the door. Gail knew at once that she had sensed something had happened.

"What is it, dear?" Mrs. Partridge said. "Tell me what has happened."

"Yes." Gail sat down beside her. "Mr. Sonny got a cut on his head, but he's going to be all right. Christopher and the doctor have taken him in for an x-ray just to make sure it's okay. And they didn't stop to tell you because they wanted to get him into a comfortable bed as fast as they could. The doctor said his pulse is a little weak but nothing alarming. No sign of another stroke."

Mrs. Partridge looked at her steadily. "How did the boy cut his head?"

For a moment Gail thought she had misunderstood, that she thought it was Christopher. But then she remembered Mrs. Partridge's disregard for time. "I did it."

Mrs. Partridge's expression didn't change. "It was an accident."

"Oh, yes! You see, the sheriff and my uncle had been chasing me. . . ." She slowed down, trying to keep calm. Her breathing was hurting her chest, and it was hard to speak without gasping. "I got away from them and saw Christopher . . . heard him singing. We climbed a big tree. Then, on the way home, he went ahead to make sure the sheriff's car was gone. I was . . . I sort of fell asleep, waiting for him, and I . . . I woke up quick because I heard someone. . . ." In spite of herself, her voice began to tremble. "I saw Mr. Sonny's arm parting the branches. He had on a long-sleeved white shirt, and for a second it looked like Uncle Chad's cast — the cast, you know, on the arm he broke. And . . . well, I was half-asleep. I mean I had been. And I threw a rock just as he came into the opening. It hit him. Hit Mr. Sonny." The tears began to stream down her face.

Mrs. Partridge leaned forward and took her hand. "My poor child."

"I could have . . . could have killed him." She put her head on her arms and sobbed.

"There, there," Mrs. Partridge murmured. "There, there. Sonny will be all right. He's been through a great deal but he survives."

"It was a terrible mistake. I thought it was. . . ."

"Of course, it was a mistake. Sometimes, the things that frighten us most are the things in our minds."

"My uncle is a wicked man. . . ."

"Well, you're with us now." She smoothed Gail's hair. "And just think, Sonny was on his way to tell you the good news."

Gail lifted her head. "What good news?"

"Why, that your father is coming."

19

HE CAME LIKE A GOD, riding a secondhand
motorcycle, his red-gold hair held back
under an electric-blue helmet. His eyes
shone with laughter and love, just as they
had before he went away. He let the motorcycle fall, its wheels still spinning. For a
moment, he and Gail looked at each other
shyly. Then he caught her up in a big hug
and whirled her around and around. The two
basenjis ran and leaped around them in a
wider circle.

He stopped and held her away from him,
looking at her. "You haven't grown up yet.
Oh, good!"

She couldn't stop giggling. "Did you think
I'd be an old lady?"

"Oh, as old as Grandma Moses or Mrs.
Methusaleh or Peter Rabbit's mother."

"*You* aren't any older at all." It was astonishing. If anything, he looked younger than she remembered him.

With his arm tight around her, he started up the path to the house. Mr. Sonny stood in the doorway, discreetly looking the other way, a big Band-aid still on his head. He had come home from the hospital three days before, and when Gail had seized his hand in both of hers to tell him how glad she was he was home and how sorry that she had hurt him, his eyes had filled with tears, he was so touched. Gail wanted to tell her father all about all of them, at once, but it would have to wait. Anyway he'd see for himself how great they were.

Mr. Sonny came toward them now, smiling. He held out his hand. "Welcome to Gail's father."

Her father shook hands warmly. "I can't tell you how grateful I am for your care of my girl."

"We have grown very fond of her."

"I hit him in the head with a rock," Gail said.

Mr. Sonny held up his hand. "It was an accident, my fault. I startled her."

Her father looked at her, puzzled. "But you don't usually fire off a rock at anybody who startles you, do you?"

She flushed. "I thought it was Uncle Chad.

He and the sheriff had been chasing me."

"But even Chad you don't throw rocks at."

"She's had a difficult time," Mr. Sonny said. "Do come in." He led the way into the kitchen and introduced Gail's father to Mrs. Partridge, who sat at the table wearing her best shawl and a ribbon in her hair.

"We love you already," Mrs. Partridge said.

He stood there, shaking his head in wonderment. "Too much!"

Mrs. Partridge nodded knowingly. "Christopher says that, too."

"Christopher is her great-grandson," Gail said. "He's the greatest."

"Will I meet him?"

"He is out in the woods just now," Mr. Sonny said, "but he promised to come home for dinner. You are, I hope — " he spoke even more slowly than usual — "going to stay with us for a time."

"I can't impose on you. You've already done so much."

"It would be a kindness to us. We seldom have visitors."

"The kind we want," Mrs. Partridge said. "We seem to get a whole landslide of sheriffs and uncles and such."

"They won't bother you anymore. I stopped to talk with my wife's doctor and with the court. It's one reason I was so slow getting here. I have custody of Gail on a temporary order, and I'm sure it will be made permanent. A notice has been sent to Chadwick. He'll accept it. He tries to do the right thing in his own peculiar way."

Gail let out a long sigh and sat down. After a minute she said, "Is Mama any better?"

He hesitated.

"You can tell me. I'm used to it."

"I know you are. You're more used to it than you should have to be. I blame myself for that. No, she isn't any better."

Later, when Mr. Sonny had made tea and brought out a plate of his lemon cookies, Gail's father said, "My wife and I were only eighteen when we got married. Much too young. Both of us suffered. I finally escaped to the South Seas brandishing my paintbrush, thinking I was the twentieth-century Gauguin. But I've learned a few things. I'm not Gauguin, for one."

"But you are good," Gail said.

"No, not good. I'm a slightly better than average second-rate painter."

"You are being modest," Mr. Sonny said.

"No, truthful. But I've got things figured out now. I'm still only thirty-four. I want to go to a university and get a teaching credential. I want to teach art in a public school."

"A teacher?" Gail was disappointed. An artist was so much more glamorous.

"Yes, sweetheart, a teacher. I think I'll enjoy it. I know I will. I like to show people how to paint."

"The thing to do this summer," Mrs. Partridge said firmly, "is to stay here and give Christopher some lessons."

"Is he an artist?"

"He's a naturalist, a very good one. But he says he is hindered because he can't handle anatomy."

"He can't draw a good frog," Gail said.

Her father laughed. "I've never studied the frog, but it shouldn't be too hard. I like anatomy."

"Then it's settled." Mrs. Partridge carefully dropped into her tea a sugar cube with a pink rosebud on it.

"But we can't take advantage like that. I thought of getting a job for the summer."

"You have your job for the summer. Christopher."

He laughed. "You are very persuasive. I love this place." He looked around. "I'd like to paint it. Both the house and the surroundings."

"We will buy your painting."

"But you don't know if you'll like them."

Gail said, "She knows a lot of things in advance."

"I have almost no money left. That's why I invaded your lovely yard on that noisy, smelly machine. I bought it in San Francisco for two hundred dollars." He paused. "Just before I got here, it occurred to me that I could have come by bus for probably one-fourth of that. You see, that's why I say I'm not a practical man."

"Artists are never practical," Mrs. Partridge said. "You can sell the motor contraption and get your money back. But it is settled, then, you will stay for the summer." She gave him a long piercing look and fell asleep.

After Sonny had put her on the bed, Gail looked at her father. "Could we?"

He spread out his hands. "I'm not a strong man. I can't resist such charming pressures."

When they showed him the room that Gail and Mr. Sonny had fixed up for him, on the second floor, he was overcome.

"It's perfect! Perfect."

It was a big room with a view of the mountains. There would be room for his painting things if he wanted to paint indoors. He sat down suddenly on the four-poster, as if his knees had given out.

"Gail, the day you fell into that empty

pool was the luckiest day of our lives!"

"Not really luck," she said. "Mrs. Partridge said it was in the Tarot cards."

"Oh, she's a Tarot person? I shall have something for her when she wakes up."

"And when you wake up," Mr. Sonny said. "You must be very tired."

"I am, rather. I drove that infernal machine all night." He touched the white embroidered pillowcase longingly.

"I will bring some hot water to the bathroom. It's two doors away."

"Let me bring it."

"No, today you are our guest." Mr. Sonny smiled. "Tomorrow you become a member of the family." He moved slowly toward the door. "Have a good rest."

Gail lingered a moment longer, hating to leave him. "Aren't they great — the Partridges?"

"Fantastic! It's hard to believe."

"I know. I didn't believe it for a long time. But it's for real."

He held out his arms. "Give me one hug before I fall asleep."

On the way downstairs she pinched herself. "Ouch!" she said aloud. Sylvester came leaping up the stairs to meet her. "He's here," she said. "Where have you been?" But maybe Sylvester had known it all the time.

20

THAT NIGHT at dinner Mr. Sonny brought up a dusty bottle of chokecherry wine that he had made himself. Gail was allowed to have a glassful. Secretly, she wasn't as enthusiastic about it as the others seemed to be, but she didn't say so.

Mr. Sonny had cooked some vegetables from his garden and he had roasted a chicken, one that Christopher had bought from a friend, they assured her; not Guinevere nor Julie Andrews nor even Miss Bullitt. And there was fresh-baked bread that "tastes like your grandmother's," Gail's father told her.

She thought of the silver spoons and the sherbet glasses. "What happened to our things?"

"They're all right. They're in storage."

She was glad. Someday she would want them. And when she had her own home, she

183

would like to have a wood-burning stove, if a person could still buy them. Mr. Sonny had taught her how to use it, and she knew how you had to use coal in winter and shake it down at night and all that. It would be nice.

Christopher and her father liked each other at once, and Christopher was enthusiastic about taking lessons in anatomical drawing.

"I'm terrible," he said. "I just can't get the hang of it. Leaves and fungi and things like that are okay, but my salamanders look like saber-toothed tigers and my frogs look like blobs of mud."

"We'll fix that. There's no great trick to it."

After dinner, her father ran upstairs to his room and brought down a book which he presented to Mrs. Partridge. "You may already have it."

She peered at it. Mr. Sonny brought her magnifying glass. After a moment she looked up, delighted. "*I Ching*! No, I don't have it. I've heard about it, of course. How very nice!" She held out her left hand to him. "You are one who knows."

"Before we get into the future," Christopher said, "let's give the present a whirl. Uncle Sonny said he'd play the piano for us. I've lighted the candles in the ballroom."

"Ballroom!" Gail's father looked at her.

"Wait till you see." She felt so proud, living in this wonderful house and showing it to her father.

Christopher carried his great-grandmother upstairs, and the others followed him. At the doorway he set her down and opened the double doors. Gail, who was just behind him, gasped. All the wall sconces held flickering candles, and the floor covering had been rolled back. Candlelight glanced off crystal and gleamed on polished wood. It was so beautiful that she could hardly stand it.

"Lo!" said Christopher. "The entrance of the gods into Valhalla."

Gail's father, who was at the end of the line and had not yet seen the room, said, "And mind you don't stub your toe on the rainbow."

Gail didn't know what they were talking about, but it was the kind of talk she liked.

Then her father stood in the doorway, stunned. "Oh!" he said softly. "Oh, I don't believe it!" He leaned against the door frame. The others moved on into the room, Mr. Sonny going to the piano, but her father still stood at the door, taking it all in. "Gail," he said. "Gail!"

"I know." She put her hand in his. "It's something else, isn't it?"

Mr. Sonny sat down and played a light rippling music, running his right hand up and down the keyboard. Christopher, who had placed his great-grandmother in a velvet chair, came back to the doorway. "Do come in. Isn't it decadent?"

Gail's father spread out his arms. "I wish I could hold it all."

Christopher smiled. "Come and be comfortable. Uncle Sonny plays well."

They sat in the gilt chairs that Christopher had arranged, next to Mrs. Partridge's armchair. Christopher sat on the floor at their feet.

For a while Mr. Sonny played. All sorts of music, some melancholy, some gay, some that Gail thought of as "intellectual." As Christopher had told her, he did most of it with his one good hand, and sometimes he hit the wrong note, shook his head in annoyance, and went on. They all sat very still, listening intently.

I no longer need a Flying Red Horse, Gail thought. I've got to the stars.

Finally, Mr. Sonny changed tempo and began a Strauss waltz. Christopher leaped up and held out his hand. "Gran? May I have the honor?"

She got to her feet a little awkwardly, but her curtsy was pure grace. "Charmed."

He held her so that her feet were off the floor, the way Gail's father used to dance with her when she was a very little girl. For a moment, they watched with delight as Christopher swayed and whirled, holding his great-grandmother in his arms. Then, Gail's father stood and said, "May I?"

She giggled. "I don't know how."

"Yes, you do. You'll see." He gathered her into his arms and began to waltz. He was right; she hardly stumbled at all. When he began to whirl, he said, "Keep looking at one thing. Then you won't get dizzy."

It was wonderful, swaying and swooping and whirling like gulls in a wind. In her mind she saw that opera company Mr. Sonny had told her about, long ago, and all those famous actors and actresses — the Barrymores and all — dancing and whirling and filling the room with color and glitter.

They exchanged partners, and she danced with Christopher, no longer afraid of stumbling, for he too held her firmly and danced with great strong steps, gliding and turning.

When Mr. Sonny stopped, smiling, they collapsed into their chairs; except Mrs. Partridge who sat up, straight and sparkling, where Gail's father had put her.

"How lovely!" she said. "We've never had a lovelier party in this old room." She looked around, as if she were seeing all the other parties, all the people.

Reluctantly they left at last, Christopher blowing out the candles carefully so as not to spatter the hot wax. In the kitchen, they had one last small glass of the chokecherry wine.

Gail's father stood and held up his glass. "To the Partridges," he said. "And to all the lovely miracles of life."

Sylvester watched from his place by the warm stove.

"I drink to my cat," Gail said, "who just might be magic."

They all raised their glasses to Sylvester. Mrs. Partridge murmured, "To magic . . ." and fell asleep.